A Kiss FOR Lucy

MONA PREVEL

DIVERSIONBOOKS

Also by Mona Prevel

Educating Emily
The Dowager's Daughter
The Love-Shy Lord

Diversion Books
A Division of Diversion Publishing Corp.
443 Park Avenue South, Suite 1008
New York, New York 10016
www.DiversionBooks.com

For more information, email info@diversionbooks.com

First Diversion Books edition April 2014.
Print ISBN: 978-1-62681-679-4
eBook ISBN: 978-1-62681-271-0

For those diamonds of the first water, my daughters-in-law, Katherine, Cynthia, Mary Ann, and for my very first critique buddy, the talented Tamara Leigh.

One

November 7, 1815 was Lucy Garwood's birthday. It did not occur to her to mention the fact to her newly acquired benefactor, the Marquess of Northwycke. Where Lucy came from, a penny's worth of bones in the stew pot might be cause for rejoicing, but birthdays? Hardly. So she spent the morning that was to change her life forever in a rose garden at Northwycke Hall, cutting flowers to adorn the table for the evening meal.

The rosebushes were bare. As she worked, their thorny branches reached out to her, plucking at her hair and smock like supplicating urchins, while chrysanthemums and asters, still blooming in a riot of color, lorded their glory over them.

Lucy liked to work in the garden, so to her delight she was allowed to pick any flowers needed for the household. As she culled the blooms, she hummed a cheerful tune that had been taught to her by her late father's friend, the pickpocket, Mickey Dempsey. It was a racy little ditty that would have had most ladies reaching for their smelling salts.

This lapse on Mickey's part had almost put an end to a friendship with her father that harked back to childhood. Despite their wretched surroundings, Josiah Garwood had imparted to Lucy all he could remember from his early childhood of the deportment of the upper classes, both in bearing and speech.

At the sound of approaching footsteps, she stopped in the middle of the refrain and silently berated herself for the lapse. *It simply will not do*, she thought. *If I am not more circumspect, I shall be sent back to London to fend for myself.* This prospect evoked a shudder.

A quick glance showed a young girl approaching. The cut of her clothes revealing a person of quality rather than a servant.

Lucy rose to her feet and shook the soil from her skirt, delaying the encounter with her as long as possible.

The girl smiled. "Good morning. You must be new here. I am Lady…"

Lucy found herself gazing into a pair of russet brown eyes regarding her in what could best be described as wide-eyed shock. She finished the sentence for her. "Maude."

"Hmm?"

"Lady Maude, I presume?"

Both girls remained rooted to the spot, each studying the other's face.

Lady Maude was the first to break the silence. "Who are you? Forgive me. If we have met prior to this, I am sure I would have remembered."

Lucy sighed. "My name is Lucy. I suspect that we were not supposed to meet, for tomorrow I am being sent to Kent to live with the younger Lady Northwycke's Aunt Hermione."

"I see," Maude replied, the look on her face belying the words. "My sister-in-law, Emily, holds her aunt in the highest regard, but your looks bespeak a kinship to *my* family, so why would they send you to live with a Walsingham?"

Lucy shrugged. "I was not told."

"May I ask what relationship you bear to me?"

Lucy fingered the gathers in the smock covering her gaunt frame. "I—er—think it would be better were you to direct that question to your brother."

"Ahem."

Both girls wheeled on hearing the deep, masculine voice.

"Most discreet of you, Lucy, my dear, but I am afraid it is far too late for that."

James Garwood, the Marquess of Northwycke, was a tall man, close to the age of thirty. Broad of shoulder, with thick dark hair falling across his forehead, and eyes the same warm brown as his sister's, he presented an attractive picture.

He gestured toward a bench. "If you would both be so kind."

Maude complied, smoothing her skirt before sitting down,

while Lucy, painfully conscious of her soiled hands and clothes, tensed, as if preparing for flight. "Perhaps it would be better were I to leave," she offered.

"No. Please sit next to Maude. She might want to ask questions—in fact, knowing my sister, that is a foregone conclusion. It is only right that you answer for yourself."

Lucy bit her lip and after a moment's hesitation sat next to Maude. She was surprised and comforted by the look of sympathy Maude accorded her. Then Maude broke the spell by rolling her eyes heavenward and exclaiming, "For goodness' sake, James, stop being so mysterious. I find it most tiresome."

Lucy was shocked by the lack of deference she showed to her brother. After all, he held one of the oldest and most illustrious titles of the realm. To her surprise, he seemed not to mind, for he gave his sister's shoulder a reassuring pat and joined them on the bench. Lucy experienced a pang of envy. How wonderful it would be to have such a brother.

James cleared his throat. "Maude, this is not easy for me." He turned to Lucy. "This is by no means a reflection on you, my dear."

"For pity's sake, James, *do* get on with it."

"Yes, please do, Uncle James. I, too, find all this most unsettling."

"*Uncle James?*" Maude sprang to her feet and faced her brother. "Lucy is our *niece?* How can this be?"

"It is so, because we had an older brother sired by our father before he married our mother. Maude, dear, I know this cannot be easy for you, but do stop hovering over me and do me the kindness of sitting down. I find your behavior most disconcerting."

Maude shrugged him off and turned her attention to Lucy. "What proof could you possibly have that your father is our brother? I had thought you to be related on our mother's side of the family—but our father's? Out of the question. Auburn hair is not a Garwood trait."

Lucy felt her bile rising. How many more Garwood females were lurking in the shadows to tear her to shreds? As far as Lucy was concerned, facing their mother, Geraldine Garwood, the older Lady Northwycke, had been more than sufficient.

She steeled herself to give a civil response. "My papa's hair, as Uncle James will verify, was almost black. It would seem that your late father had a fondness for beautiful ladies with auburn hair. My grandmama also had that shade."

"I declare, such a taradiddle! Why have we not heard of this brother before? This must be a scheme of that rascal, Mickey Dempsey. I do not care how marvelous he is with horses, talking to them, indeed; Mama was right, it was absolute madness to trust him."

"But you have heard of our brother," James replied. "He was the one called Gentleman Joe, the consumptive highwayman who died during the ill-conceived raid on the *Ocean Queen*, earlier this year."

"My father was a rag-and-bone man, as well you know, Uncle James. He lacked the stomach for being a road agent."

"Forgive the embellishment, Lucy. Since he rode the highway for a short while, I made the story as romantic as possible for my sister, I had no idea at the time that Gentleman Joe was our brother."

"Josiah. My father was always called Josiah at home. He preferred to put his days as a highwayman behind him."

"Forgive me, child. I shall remember that."

Maude placed both hands on her hips. "Are you telling me that it was *our* father who dragged his son out of boarding school and abandoned him to the tender mercies of a band of pickpockets? It is too horrid to contemplate."

James nodded. "He doubted the boy's paternity."

"But even so, James, surely he must have developed *some* affection for Josiah. To abandon an innocent child to a life of degradation is absolutely unforgivable."

"Our mother was of the same opinion."

"Really?" Maude plucked a withered rose leaf still clinging to an otherwise bare branch. With scarcely a glance she cast it to the ground. "Then Mama agrees with you on this? There is no doubt at all?"

"None whatsoever. I was going to tell you about it when the time was right."

"And when would that have been, pray tell? When Lucy was bundled off to Emily's Aunt Hermione? Or perhaps you intended to wait until we were all old and doddering."

James frowned. "Now, Maude, such an outburst is most unseemly of you. I know it is a shock, but perhaps it is just as well it is out in the open."

"Then there is no need to send Lucy away."

James shrugged. "What do you suggest that we do with her? I do not wish for her circumstances to come to light. It is strictly the concern of our family. When she is of an age, I intend to see her married to a decent gentleman, who of course will be privy to her background, but no one else will be the wiser."

Maude turned to Lucy. "Have you had any say in the matter?"

"Uncle James has assured me that I do not have to marry where my heart does not lie."

"Has he indeed?" She flashed her brother a look of scorn. "And if her heart is never engaged, is she supposed to live out her days dancing attention on an elderly dowager? Swept under a rug, like so much unwelcome dirt?"

"Maude, that is quite enough. The very idea."

"No. It is not enough, James. Why cannot Lucy stay here? She could share my governess and dancing master." She addressed Lucy. "Would you not like to be my friend and learn how to how to dance?"

For a moment, Lucy's spirits soared. Having a friend sounded wonderful. Then she crashed to earth. "It is not for me to decide."

James gave her what she interpreted to be a contemplative look, then caved in. "The final decision has to be Mother's. This whole affair has been most distressing for her."

Maude gave a little skip. "Then it is all settled, for I am certain Mama will agree to it."

James stroked his chin. "I do believe you are right. Mother seems to have an inability to deny you anything, you little minx."

Maude clapped her hands. "Then Lucy shall join us for

dinner this evening, and help me celebrate my birthday."

Lucy gave a tiny gasp. "Today is your birthday, Lady Maude?"

"Yes, my sixteenth."

"How extraordinary. It is my birthday too, only I am fifteen."

Maude's eyes widened. "Really?" Her face crinkled with delight. "That will make it all the jollier. But please, if we are to be friends, you must call me Maude."

"Your ladyship, I could not presume."

"Nonsense. I refuse to call you Miss Garwood and under no circumstances shall I allow you to address me as Aunt Maude, so there you have it."

Lucy felt a rising glow. "Very well, Lady Maude."

"Maude, just Maude."

"You are right." James stroked his chin. "Aunt Maude is out of the question, and so is Uncle James. Why did I not catch that? As we are to be distant cousins, it should be Cousin Maude and Cousin Northwycke, I suppose."

Maude shook her head. "Northwycke is far too stuffy. I prefer Cousin James."

James shrugged. "Very well. I doubt anyone will care."

It had been several weeks since Maude had convinced her mother to allow Lucy to stay. Maude had proved to be a generous, warm-hearted friend. Although there were times Lucy wished she had not offered to share her dancing lessons.

As Lucy struggled to follow the instructions of the dancing master one morning, she railed at her own clumsiness.

The dancing master shook his head. "Lightly, lightly, Miss Garwood. No, no. The toe, she must be pointed thus."

Lucy felt wretched. Try as she might, she could not satisfy the graceful Frenchman. Maude played the lively quadrille with considerable brio while her mother kept the beat with her lorgnette, so Lucy could not fault the music. To make matters worse, James Garwood entered the music room and stood beside the dowager, who greeted him without missing a beat.

"What seems to be the problem?" he asked. "Granted,

Lucy's style seems to be a trifle stilted, but it is passable. Not every young lady is fortunate enough to be endowed with your grace, Mother."

She indulged in a preening smile. "I suppose you are right. But even so…"

Lucy was mortified by their words. To make matters worse, she stumbled and a sharp pain lanced through her foot, causing her to wince.

"For heaven's sake, no wonder her dancing leaves much to be desired, there is something wrong with her foot." He signaled Maude to stop playing. "Lucy," he called, "have the goodness to come over here."

Lucy limped toward the piano. "Yes, Cousin James?"

"Your foot, child. It seems to be bothering you. It would be prudent to have Dr. Mainwaring look at it."

"Oh, no!" Lucy raised her hand to her mouth, aware of an embarrassed heat that surely had turned her face beet red. "There is nothing wrong with my foot."

James frowned. "Nonsense. It is obviously causing you considerable distress." He patted her back. "Come, child. There is nothing to be afraid of. Dr. Mainwaring is not a leech given to parting his patients from their blood at the slightest excuse."

Lucy squared her shoulders. "I am not afraid of such a paltry thing, Cousin James. Only…" She found it impossible to continue.

He raised her chin with his thumb and forefinger. "Lucy, my dear, we are your family and will always do what is best for you."

A lump rose in her throat. It was all she could do to keep the tears from flowing. "You have all been so incredibly kind, how could I possibly voice any complaint about the beautiful dancing slippers Maude so generously gave to me?"

"My slippers?" Maude interjected. "But I loved them. I was sorry when they became too small for me." She paused. "Oh, dear. I see. They do not fit you either. For pity's sake, why did you not say something?"

"Yes, indeed. Why not?" The dowager gave her head an impatient toss. "Small wonder your dancing is so abysmal.

Remove them immediately and replace them with your walking shoes."

James shook his head, "I do not think it will help, Mother. I rather suspect the rest of the shoes we gave to Lucy fit her no better. Is that not correct, dear?"

Lucy nodded.

"Perhaps a pair of mine will suffice until we get her to a shoemaker," his mother suggested.

"She needs more than a visit to the shoemaker," James replied. "We are not paupers. Since you have already planned a trip to the city next week to refurbish Maude's wardrobe, I would deem it a kindness if you would allow Lucy to accompany you."

"Oh?"

"Yes, if you would. See to it that she is suitably outfitted as becomes a young lady of my household. I cannot for the life of me understand how I came to overlook this matter."

Lucy fought back her tears. "Please, Cousin James, you are far, far too good to me as it is." She turned to the dowager. "You also, madam. I sincerely hope I never give you cause to regret your kindness."

The dowager inclined her head. "I should hope not. But then, human nature being what it is, that is all anyone can do. For your sake, Lucy, I hope you never conduct yourself in a manner that would give our family cause for shame or in any way jeopardize your own future happiness."

Lucy nodded. "Not only is such an idea odious to me, madam, it is my sincere desire to conduct myself in a manner which will inspire approval in others and pride in those who bear the Garwood name."

"Hmmph! A lofty sentiment to be sure." She turned to her son. "Kindly see that Lucy is ready to leave at first light Monday morning. The days are short this time of year." She placed a hand on Maude's shoulder. "That is enough dancing for today. It is time we went home."

"Please, Mama, I would like to stay for a while and visit with Emily and Lucy."

"Very well, although I doubt Emily is up to the task of

receiving you. The poor darling is still indisposed by the early months of her delicate condition."

"Then she will improve?"

"Eventually. It is something ladies have to endure at such times. Please be home for luncheon." With a brief nod to James she departed for the Dower House.

Presently the sound of her horse and gig faded into the distance. Maude gave an almost imperceptible sigh. "You must not mind Mama, Lucy. She is known for speaking her mind. I rather think she likes you, but would probably choke on the words before admitting it."

"Now, Maude, that is no way to speak of Mother."

"But it is true. I mean no disrespect. I love Mama, but you know perfectly well she is not one to mince her words."

"If it comes to that, my darling sister, you do not exactly dance around issues either."

Maude shrugged. "I suppose we both lack the patience for humbug." She turned to Lucy. "I am so glad you are coming to London with us. We shall have a splendid time."

Lucy felt a surge of excitement. With Maude for a companion, how could a visit to London not be?

Two

Lucy accompanied Maude and her mother to London in a magnificent dark green carriage. She nestled into its rich upholstery in absolute awe of its grandeur, convinced that dukes of the blood-royal owned none finer.

Having always been obliged to do most of her traveling on foot, it had been Lucy's experience that if one wished not to be muddied, or maimed, such a grand conveyance was something to avoid. Not in her wildest imaginings had she ever pictured herself as a passenger in one. It seemed that in a twinkling of an eye the impossible had come to pass.

She looked back on the circumstances following the death of her father and shuddered. The dowager gave her a questioning look. "Is something the matter?" she asked.

"No, I thank you, Madam. I must have nodded off for the moment."

Lucy shrank deeper into the fur robe covering her lap, resolving not to draw any more attention from that quarter. She closed her eyes and, as she leaned against the seat, reviewed the tragic events leading up to the sudden rise in her fortune.

Lucy and her mother had been reduced to working for a mantuamaker under the most wretched of circumstances. Quick to appreciate the fine needlework of Lucy's mother, and even quicker to take advantage of their desperate plight, the woman had driven a shrewd bargain. For a pittance in wages and a meager ration of food, they had been accorded the privilege of sleeping in the same drafty attic in which they toiled long hours, sewing clothes for more fortunate women.

The poor food and unsatisfactory sleeping conditions soon took their toll on her mother's health and within two months she had succumbed to a severe case of lung fever. From that point Lucy's plight had become unbearable.

"Your mother's death changes the situation," the mantuamaker had said, her lips pressed into a hard, thin line. "Naturally, I cannot continue to pay you anything. Your services are scarcely worth the food you consume, but from the goodness of my heart, I shall keep you in my employ and you may continue to sleep in the workroom."

Still numb from seeing her mother's body interred in a pauper's grave, and having nowhere else to go, Lucy acquiesced.

Her employer indicated a woman standing in the doorway. "You will share the room with Miss Harris. She will fill your mother's position and is to be obeyed in all things, unless I say otherwise."

"As you wish, ma'am," Lucy replied with a curtsy.

The new seamstress, a tall, gaunt creature with stringy, dishwater-colored hair, gave Lucy an assessing stare, then addressed the proprietress. "Impudent little baggage. Aping her betters with such airs and graces. Can't see as she'd be much use in a sewing room. I 'ave a little sister at 'ome in need of employment who'd be far more suitable."

"That will do, Miss Harris. I am in charge here, if you don't mind. As long as Lucy does her work, there will be no changes."

As soon as their employer was downstairs and out of earshot, Miss Harris wheeled on Lucy, her gray eyes coldly hostile. "Mark my words, you fancy little cow, by the end of the week you'll find starving in the gutter much better than working 'ere." She punctuated this remark with a vicious punch to Lucy's arm.

Actually, it only took two days of pinching, punching, and needle jabbing before Lucy rebelled against the abuse. Without so much as gathering her meager belongings, she departed the premises, but not before dumping a bowl of watery cabbage soup over her tormentor's head.

Lucy ran as fast as her feet would carry her, firmly convinced that if she was caught she would be hauled before a magistrate and some dire punishment meted out. She did not slow the pace until the pain in her lungs outweighed the fear of capture, finally coming to a halt at the entrance to a park.

Suddenly, she was aware of the disapproving looks of passersby. She smoothed her hair and entered the park through the black wrought-iron gates with an assumed air of nonchalance. This façade quickly melted, for she had scarcely set foot on the pathway when a masculine voice called out, "Lucy?"

She almost fell to her knees.

"It *is* you. Criminy, girl, you know better than to be roamin' around London all by yourself."

It was Lucy's turn to express disbelief. "Mickey Dempsey? How can this be?" She beheld the man. His clothes were worn, but clean, as was he, giving one the impression of shabby gentility, yet his manner of speaking proclaimed him to be a denizen of one of the lowlier parts of the city.

"Your fortunes must have changed for the better. You look absolutely splendid. I suppose one ought to address you as Mr. Dempsey, now. How came you by your good fortune?"

The man preened. "I do, don't I? Regular tulip, as the gentry says. But before I go into that, suppose you tell me whatcha think your doing, traipsin' all over London by yourself? I 'ave a 'ard time believing your mum knows what you're about."

"Alas, poor Mama passed away but three days ago." Her lower lip began to quiver. "Th-they buried her in a pauper's grave."

Mickey Dempsey patted her shoulder. "There, there, love. Don't take on so."

"But she is all alone. She should be with Papa." Her tears flowed freely.

"And so she shall be."

"You are in a position to rectify the matter?"

"No, love. Can't say as I am. But Lord Northwycke will oblige, I'm sure."

"Lord Northwycke?"

"The gent what buried your dad at St. Anne's."

"Ah, yes. A marquess, I believe?"

"One and the same."

"Tell me, Mickey, what moved such a personage to interest

himself in Papa's affairs?"

"The gentry are a strange lot. I suppose 'aving your dad die at his feet during that skirmish on his ship upset him. Then when I told him about the both of us being raised by a band of pickpockets an' all, you should 'ave seen the look on 'is face. I thought 'e was going to burst out crying."

Lucy felt the blood drain from her face. "How can you tell such lies?" She shook her fist at him. "My papa died in his own bed. Do not try to drag him down to your own level."

"Criminy. Forgive me, Lucy. I could cut my tongue out for upsetting you so. My mistake, I took an 'eavy blow to the 'ead that night, and I'm not sure just what did 'appen."

Recognizing the words that had slipped past Mickey's guard to be the truth, Lucy felt drained. She slumped onto a nearby bench. "No, Mickey. It is time for me to know what really took place. Why, oh why, did Papa engage in such a perfidious act? Joining the dregs of the docks in raiding a respectable merchant ship. And you, too, for that matter. What were you thinking? You both must have been mad."

Mickey gave her a sheepish grin. "I've thought the same thing. An enemy of Lord Northwycke's was willing to pay a lot of money to make sure that cargo was stolen, and your dad was sorely in need of the ready. I went along to keep an eye on 'im."

"I find it difficult to believe my father would seek the ruin of another man, no matter how much someone was willing to pay. He did not have the stomach for such things."

"Ordinarily I'd agree with you, but Joe knew 'e was dying, and 'e wanted to leave something to tide 'is family over. If the raid 'ad been successful, your mum would most likely still be alive and you wouldn't be dashing all over the place in such a shameful fashion."

He gave a few disapproving tuts, then added, "You never *did* say what you was about."

She gave an account of what had taken place. As her tale unfolded, Mickey's brow furrowed and his fists clenched until his knuckles turned white. "I'd like to get my 'ands on that bloodsucker. She murdered your poor mum just as surely as if she'd taken a knife to 'er."

"No, Mickey. It would serve no purpose and would most certainly earn both of us a trip to the gallows."

The tension was broken when she came to her anointing of the malevolent Miss Harris with the cabbage soup. Mickey roared with laughter and slapped his thigh. "Well done, young Lucy. Though I think you did well to run. There's no saying what them two 'ags might 'ave done to yer. Evil pair o' bitches."

Mickey's delivery was loud, his laughter hearty, earning disapproving glances from several passersby. Lucy felt embarrassed to be in his company, then experienced remorse for feeling so. Mickey had a generous heart and over the years had proven too good a friend to the Garwoods to warrant such disloyalty. She dismissed her thoughts. "You have yet to tell me how you came by your good fortune."

"I've Lord Northwycke to thank fer that. I 'appened to run into 'im at the docks, an' 'e was kind enough to let me tend to 'is 'orses while 'e saw 'is ship off."

"How very singular of him to trust an admitted pickpocket with what was undoubtedly very fine horseflesh."

Mickey nodded. "I didn't 'alf get the wind up, too. Sort of wished I'd kept my mouth shut. I'd've been in a right 'ow d'ya do, if some of the dock scum 'd seen fit to 'elp themselves to 'em."

"I assume it is safe to say this did not occur?"

"You 'ave the right of it. In fact, 'is lordship was proper pleased with the way I 'andled 'is cattle. Gave me a fistful 'o coins, in fact. I just shoved 'em in me pocket, thinking they was pennies." Mickey smiled, as if savoring the moment. "It warn't till I got 'ome, I found they was sovereigns."

"Like a dream come true. I admire the way you saw fit to improve your appearance, it bespeaks a wonderful sense of pride."

Mickey looked rueful. "Now then, Lucy, it sounds very nice, but I'm no 'umbug. I got cleaned up to improve my trade."

"To improve your trade? I do not understand."

"I wished to mingle with a more likely crowd. Might

as well be 'anged fer cuttin' the purse of a gent as that of a costermonger."

He threw his shoulders back and assumed an air of bravado, rather like a small boy whistling in the dark to deny his fear. Lucy was not deceived. She knew only too well that the specter of death on the gibbet was a constant companion to those who followed Mickey's path.

She touched his shoulder. "I wish there was some other way, Mickey. It is only a matter of time before you are caught."

"Don't you go worrying your 'ead about me, young Lucy. I can outrun any of these overfed gents any day of the week." He jingled the coins, bulging his pockets, and gave an amply girthed aristocrat, who happened to be passing by, a contemptuous glance. "In fact, if this keeps up, I'll be able to pack it in, buy a little 'ouse. Grow my own vegetables an' all."

A bone-jarring jolt caused by the carriage rattling over a large pothole brought Lucy back to her present situation.

"Really!" the dowager expostulated while hastily adjusting her bonnet. "I have a good mind to give Jones a thorough set-down for such careless handling of the ribbons. I must be bruised from head to foot."

After her initial outburst and the straightening of her bonnet, she assumed an air of stony-faced silence. Maude's only acknowledgment of the shake-up was to assume an upright position once more, a rueful smile quirking her lips and a frown furrowing her brow.

Lucy forbore the temptation to rub her bottom. Evidently there was more to being a lady than the possession of a well-modulated accent.

Will I ever belong? she wondered. There was such a gap between the classes. She recalled how James Garwood had confided that when Mickey had turned up at Northwycke Hall with herself in tow, he had been touched by the transformation in Mickey's appearance, venturing the opinion that his new clothes and his cleanliness were in deference to his rank. Knowing otherwise, she had been hard put to keep from laughing at such delusion. As for as she was concerned, her uncle need never know that Mickey had

had more venal reasons for braving the horrors of a bathhouse.

The carriage veered sharply around a corner, slamming Lucy's head to the side. She was grateful for the heavily padded squabs adorning the carriage interior. Up till that point she had assumed the green and gold velvet upholstery to be merely ostentatious decoration; now she realized they prevented one's brains from being separated from one's skull. It seemed that being a member of the aristocracy was fraught with its own peculiar forms of peril.

The older woman muttered under her breath. Lucy assumed it bode no good for the feckless driver. To her surprise, Maude's face was wreathed in smiles.

"Oh, look!" she exclaimed, leaning forward to grab Lucy's arm. "We have arrived. Is not Northwycke House a most handsome edifice?"

Lucy peered out the window. Behind a pair of huge wrought iron gates soared a graceful pile of stone and glass. "House? It is called Northwycke House? Oh, Maude. Such a name is inadequate. It is a palace fit for a princess."

The dowager raised a brow. "You must refrain from such extravagant statements, child, lest those in polite society assume you are unaccustomed to their milieu."

Before Lucy could respond, the older Lady Northwycke was helped from the carriage by Jones, who was promptly rewarded for his trouble with a swat of her lorgnette and a few choice words concerning the recklessness of his driving.

Before alighting the carriage, Maude gave Lucy a sympathetic smile. "You must not mind Mama, she wants to make sure that you secure the best place possible in society."

"If such a place exists for me," Lucy muttered as she stepped down.

Maude turned around. "I am sorry, Lucy dear, I did not quite catch what you said."

"It was of no import. I merely remarked that there must be so much to see."

"Quite so," Maude replied with a warm smile. "And we shall begin with a visit to the mantuamaker first tiling tomorrow."

• • •

The mantuamaker's was the third place they called on the next morning, Clark and Debenham being the first. Lucy was stunned by the quantity of stockings and undergarments Maude's mother deemed necessary for her to have. Their next stop was the shop of a shoemaker on the lower end of Bond Street, who, to Lucy's surprise, actually measured her feet before producing an assortment of fine kid slippers for her to try on.

The dowager supervised the proceedings, her head cocked to one side, either nodding her approval, or shaking her head as Lucy displayed each pair on her narrow feet. Lucy held her breath as she showed off a particularly fashionable pair of sandals which criss-crossed over her slender calves in the Roman style, hoping against hope that they would meet with the older woman's approval, but was disappointed when the lady pursed her lips and shook her head.

"Do let Lucy have them, Mama," Maude remonstrated. "She is one of the few people with ankles trim enough to do them justice."

"Really, Maude, such an outburst is most unseemly. Besides, those things are scarcely serviceable."

"But, dearest mama, what could it hurt? I expect that Lucy has never had the opportunity to be frivolous in her entire life."

Lucy watched as Maude gave her mother a most beseeching look with her beautiful, russet brown eyes. To her surprise the lady seemed to melt under their spell.

It must be marvelous to have such beguiling ways, she thought. Then she remembered that she, too, possessed a pair of fine brown eyes. She had not thought them to be so until she had seen eyes of the same shape and color enhancing Maude's striking features. Indeed, until she had beheld Maude it had not occurred to her that she had the slightest chance of ever being considered pretty. Now, Lucy knew that if she could add a little flesh to her bones there was a distinct possibility…

She gave a hopeless shrug. *No matter how much I resemble Maude*, she thought, *I will never possess her charm—that, and a generous heart, are the true key to her beauty.*

Not wanting her friend's mother to be pressured into buying the sandals, and thereby indirectly incurring her wrath, Lucy said, "They are very beautiful, Maude, and it is very kind of you to speak up for me, but your mama is right, they are not suitable."

This pretty statement earned Lucy an approving glance. "You are quite right, of course, child. A trifle too sophisticated for one so young. Next year, they will be far more suitable." The dowager turned to the shoemaker. "Kindly measure Miss Garwood for boots. A pair of half boots in brown, and some riding boots in black, and see that they are delivered to Northwycke House as soon as possible."

"R—riding boots?" Terror clutched Lucy's heart. The only horse she'd had dealings with was Daisy, a rundown mare who had hauled her father's rag-and-bone cart all over London. She used to feed the horse an occasional carrot that had been intended for the stew pot, but had never been astride her, and had not wished to be. This was the result of being knocked down as a young child by a carelessly handled horse.

The dowager drew in her breath. "But of course it is hardly likely that you would have had the benefit of riding lessons." She dismissed the matter with an impatient wave. "Never mind, that will soon be remedied."

Lucy opened her mouth to voice protest, but changed her mind. She had resided at Northwycke Hall long enough to know that once the lady made up her mind about something, she was scarcely likely to change it, unless for a beseeching plea from Maude.

A footman placed their packages in the carriage, and they walked the few yards it took to reach the mantuamaker. Lucy froze with fear as she recognized the shop in which she and her mother had slaved, but to her relief before they reached it they turned into a much nicer-looking establishment. A small, birdlike woman with a high, rounded bosom and very narrow hips rushed over to greet them. "Lady Northwycke, it is an honor to serve such an august personage," she gushed.

"Lord preserve me," the dowager muttered under her breath.

Once they were seated, she lost no time in making her needs known. "Mrs. Eliot, kindly pay close attention to what I have to say, as we have a lot to cover and I do not wish to be here all day."

"Indeed?" Mrs. Eliot's expression could best be described as avid.

"Indeed. My daughter, Lady Maude, and her—er cousin, Miss Garwood, need to be measured for morning gowns, carriage dresses, and, of course, evening dresses. I think we should include a riding habit for Miss Garwood."

Mrs. Eliot clapped her hands, her nose twitching with excitement. A sturdy-looking assistant put in an appearance, and at her mistress's behest brought in a succession of materials from finest muslins and silks to merinos and broadcloth. Mrs. Eliot absented herself from the room to supervise the acquisition of some taffetas for their perusal.

The dowager used the time to hold a fine kerseymere in a shade of apple green to Lucy's face. "Hmm. Yes. Most becoming."

"It is lovely, madam, but ought I not to be in mourning for my Mama and Papa?" Lucy's voice was barely above a whisper.

"Alas, child, we cannot bring that much attention to the matter," the dowager whispered in response. "No Garwoods have met their demise for quite some time. It is best we remain quite vague as to which branch of the family you belong. Unfortunately, a come-out will be quite out of the question for you, so I doubt anyone will be overly concerned."

The return of Mrs. Eliot, accompanied by her assistant bearing several bolts of cloth, brought the conversation to an abrupt halt. The dowager fingered a sky blue watered silk. "This will make you a lovely spencer jacket for the white sarcenet dress you have, Maude dear."

To Lucy's awe, the lady made her selections with amazing rapidity as a variety of materials and corresponding patterns passed through her hands. Lucy could find no fault with the choices she made. She had impeccable taste. It seemed that

Maude agreed, because save for the odd difference as to color preference, she went along with her mother's choices.

At the conclusion, the dowager said, "Very well, Mrs. Eliot, this day next month a carriage will be sent for you, and I shall expect you at Northwycke Hall for the final fittings."

"N—Northwycke Hall? But, your ladyship, that is so far, and I have my poor establishment to run."

The Dowager Marchioness of Northwycke rose to her feet. It was a deliberate majestic gesture. "Nonsense!" Her voice crackled with frost. "Of course, if you are unable to cope with an undertaking of such magnitude, kindly say so. There are plenty of others who would be only too glad to oblige."

Mrs. Eliot twittered her assurances. A look of grim satisfaction flitted across the dowager's face. "I rather thought so. Remember, this day next month the carriage will be here to pick you up at seven o'clock sharp. Kindly be ready."

"The effrontery of the creature," she muttered once they were on the street. "One would think for an order of that size she would be on her hands and knees thanking the Lord for her good fortune."

Before Maude or Lucy could offer an opinion, a nearby church clock struck two. "My goodness," Lady Northwycke remarked, "I had no idea it was so late. No wonder I am hungry. I do believe a visit to Gunter's is called for."

Robert Renquist, the seventh Duke of Linborough, was a tall young man whose broad shoulders, granite jaw, and close-cropped fair hair made him look unapproachable, yet he had spent a thoroughly tedious morning squiring his mother to the usual round of "at homes."

He derived no pleasure from visiting rouged dowagers who held court in their bedchambers, where the order of the day was to tear to shreds the reputations of the unfortunate members of the *ton* who had not seen fit to attend their deadly affairs. Unfortunately, he could not find it in his heart to deny his mother an escort.

It would be nice to think that this was because his large, incredibly vivid blue eyes, bespoke a tender heart, but this was not entirely the case. Her Grace had a gift for reducing Robert and his sisters, Lady Esther, and Lady Miriam, to such quivering masses of guilt Machiavelli would have paid homage at her feet.

No parent since the dawn of time had done so much for her children, and when it suited her purpose a litany to her sacrifices would ripple off her tongue with amazing rapidity. If this did not move her children to do her bidding, the graphic details of the agony she had so bravely endured to bring them into the world would. Over the years this ploy had inspired such terror in the bosoms of Lady Esther and Lady Miriam they turned down suitors with alarming regularity and were fast approaching spinsterhood.

After departing the last house, Robert helped his mother into the family carriage, a handsome equipage in a deep burgundy with a menacing-looking griffon with a coronet above its head emblazoned on its doors.

He carefully arranged a robe of beaver fur on her lap and was rewarded with a smile. There was a time many a man would have sold his soul for one of Martha Renquist's smiles. Even though her blonde beauty was fast fading, her smile was still a delicious combination of fine, even teeth and dimpled cheeks.

"Thank you for my outing, Robert dear," she cooed. Her eyes registered a look that could best be described as a mixture of motherly love and unspoken gratitude.

Robert braced himself for whatever demand was sure to follow.

"I think a visit to Gunter's would be a perfect ending to the social round. Do you not agree?"

"For pity's sake, Mother, you partook of refreshments in every house we visited."

"A mere nibble here and there, Robert. Most of the food was scarcely fit for the palate of one of my sensibilities." Her lips formed a moue. "Of course, if it is too much trouble to indulge your lady mother in such a trifle…" Her bosom heaved. "Heaven knows I have spoiled all of my children. No sacrifice on my part has been too great."

Without bothering to reply, Robert rapped the roof of the carriage and called to the driver, "Gunter's, if you please."

Once seated at one of the desirable window tables, the duchess gave her son a nudge in the ribs. "I declare, Geraldine Garwood just came through the door, and, if I am not mistaken, she has her daughter, Maude, in tow. I wonder who the scrawny little creature is they have with them?"

Robert cast a jaundiced eye toward the door. "I cannot for the life of me understand why the arrival of the Garwoods should be cause for so much excitement."

"No, I do not suppose you can. You are far too interested in pursuing your own selfish pleasures to concern yourself with your duty toward your family."

"I suppose you are referring to your desire to see me leg-shackled."

His mother frowned, causing a network of fine wrinkles to deepen across her forehead. "Please do not use such deplorable language, Robert. It is so vulgar."

"Surely you do not have the Northwycke dowager's chit in mind for my future duchess?"

"She has impeccable bloodlines and comes with a handsome dowry. There are not too many families one can deem worthy of an alliance with ours, my darling."

Robert could scarcely contain his rising indignation. "You go too far, Mother. Lady Maude is a mere child. Surely you do not expect me to rob the cradle?"

"The girl has had her sixteenth birthday, and will have her come-out next Season."

Robert smiled and leaned back in his chair. "Then there is no hurry, is there? In the meantime, I shall relax, and savor my freedom a while longer."

Her Grace raised her eyes heavenward. "What did I do to deserve such a paperscull for a son? Do you not realize that by then it may well be too late? A handsome girl of great fortune will have every available bachelor swarming around her the very first day of her come-out."

"Sounds like a hopeless cause to me."

"You are playing the noddy to drive me mad. I insist you cultivate her friendship this instant." She beckoned to a waitress who was hovering nearby. "Kindly invite Lady Northwycke to share our table, if you please."

Robert rose to greet the dowager and her charges. Lady Northwycke inclined her head in a most regal manner toward the duchess. "Your Grace." Then to her son. "Your Grace. Such a kind invitation. I believe you already know my daughter, Lady Maude."

Maude curtsied, and accorded each an honorific.

Robert was relieved that she did not simper, but gave him a slight smile before lowering her gaze in a genteel manner.

"Allow me to present Miss Garwood."

The girl curtsied, and muttered something unintelligible.

The duchess gave Lucy a keen perusal with her quizzing glass. "One of the Shrewsbury cousins, I presume?"

Lady Northwycke gave the duchess a brief smile and the merest of nods.

Robert gallantly helped to seat his guests, then called for an assortment of pastries and ices.

While they were partaking of the ices, he noticed that the wraithlike Miss Garwood's eyes gleamed with pleasure, yet she was most diffident in her attitude, and not once contributed to the conversation, unless posed a direct question. He was also quick to notice that Lady Northwycke hastily answered any question involving her family. He attributed the young girl's gaucherie to extreme youth, and a life spent in Shropshire, one of the more rustic of the shires.

Lady Maude, on the other hand, joined in the conversation with an animated enthusiasm without the slightest trace of shyness, or guile. Robert was not entirely sure this was a good thing. A little reticence sometimes saved one a lot of grief.

"I understand you are to have your come-out next Season," he offered, curious as to her reaction to this subject.

"Quite so, Your Grace. I am looking forward to it so much. I expect it will be most jolly."

"You think so, Lady Maude? I rather thought a come-out was a very serious endeavor."

"Really?" Maude frowned, as if perplexed. "In what way, Your Grace?"

"The whole point of having a Season is to acquire a spouse. The choices you make in the next year or so, or those made for you, will determine whether or not you have a life of unmitigated misery, sheer bliss, or something in between."

To Robert's surprise, she burst out laughing. A pleasant musical sound, he noted.

"La, Your Grace, one would think you were trying to scare me into a nunnery."

Robert smothered a laugh. Lady Maude was too innocent to know the darker meaning of such a word. "And you are not so easily intimidated?"

"I have no reason to be. In the first place, my brother is an enlightened man who would not force me into an arranged marriage, and I, sir, would willingly embrace a life of spinsterhood rather than marry where my heart does not lie."

Robert inclined his head. "I stand corrected, Lady Maude. Life does indeed hold no fears for you."

He noticed the younger girl seemed not to respond to any of the conversation being conducted, but stolidly waded through the delectables that were placed before her. He wondered how a girl whose bones seemed to stick through her clothes could eat so much.

It struck him as odd. Both girls bore a remarkable resemblance to each other, yet were so different. Both had the classic features of Greek statuary. Flat, smooth brows, straight noses, sensually sculptured mouths, and firm chins. The visages of goddesses, crowned by a glorious abundance of auburn hair.

It was a shame. Lady Maude seemed destined to become a diamond of the first water, and her country cousin would, most likely, always resemble a scrawny kitten. It was bad enough the younger girl lacked charm and grace. Did she have to compound it by proving to be such a dull little creature with no opinions of her own? Something contrary in his nature goaded him into baiting her.

"What say you, Miss Garwood? Would you refuse to marry a man of your family's choosing?"

"That would depend, Your Grace."

"On what? His face? His fortune? His disposition?"

She looked him squarely in the eye. "Those are strange questions for a gentleman to be asking, although I must admit that I have never been in the company of a duke before, and in this I could be mistaken."

Robert was taken aback. Evidently, the girl could hold her own. A brave creature with a forthright spirit. He felt remorse for having put her in such a position. "You are quite right, of course. My apologies, Miss Garwood."

"I am of the same opinion as Lady Maude."

"Hmm?"

"You asked me what would induce me to marry. That is simple. I would only marry where my heart lies, and even then, I would only marry a man who loved me in return, so in all probability shall remain a spinster."

On the journey back to the ducal mansion, which happened to be situated close to the square where Northwycke House was situated, his mother raised the subject. "Thank heaven Lady Maude is the one endowed with all the feminine charm, and not her cousin. Have you ever encountered such a graceless country mouse?"

"You underestimate the young lady, Mother. Granted, she lacks the feminine graces, but she is far from being a mouse. Did you see how she stood up to me?"

"How could I not? She had no respect for your rank, whatsoever. Impudent little chit. 'Marry where her heart lies,' indeed. Who would want to be saddled with such a creature?"

Robert smiled. "I doubt she will have trouble finding a mate."

His mother raised a brow. "Really? Come now, Robert, surely you jest?"

He shook his head. "Granted, The Shrewsbury Garwoods are a bloodless lot. The result of too much intermarriage in that particular branch of the family, I fear, but they are inordinately rich. I am sure the size of Miss Garwood's dowry will make her very lovable in the eyes of *some* young man."

Three

Lady Northwycke remained unusually silent during the carriage ride home from Gunter's. Then, as soon as the three of them entered the reception hall to Northwycke House, she said, "It behooves us to stay home tomorrow. We were seen by enough people of our acquaintance today, who know that when I am in Town, I am in the habit of receiving callers on Wednesdays."

Maude pulled a face. "But surely there is no need for Lucy and I to stay home. I was *so* looking forward to buying some new handkerchiefs, and I *desperately* need to replace the lace on some of my things."

"You little pea-goose. Do you not realize the significance of our encounter with the Renquists?"

"What are you saying, Mama? All we did was eat a few pastries and some ices. Of course, there was that ridiculous conversation concerning come-outs, and husband catching, the Duke of Linborough, insisted on pursuing. It was most odd, to say the least."

"Of a certainty, the Duchess instigated the invitation to share their table, and you may be sure, it was not to marvel at your conversational brilliance."

"Then why did she invite us, Mama?"

"Because she wanted her son to become aware of your existence. I believe the puffed-up creature might actually consider you worthy of becoming the next Duchess of Linborough." Her voice was tinged with irony. "For the daughter of a lowly curate, she is very concerned over the lineage of others."

Maude's eyes widened. "A curate's daughter? Surely not? I have heard she is very high in the instep, and gives the cut direct to anyone she considers unworthy of her condescension."

31

"Nevertheless, the duchess came from humble parentage. She lived on the estate next to that of my family. Indirectly, she owes her rise in fortune due to the fact the late duke literally ran into her while attending a foxhunt my father was hosting. Even as a girl she was clever and manipulative. That, and her extraordinary beauty, made the duke easy prey. To this day, she has her family dancing attention with her clever little ploys." Her mother smiled. "Rest assured, her son *will* call to pay his respects on the morrow."

"How perfectly horrid. Last summer, lest I should entertain a *tendre* for Emily's brother, you tried to foist one of Lord Crestwood's odious sons upon me."

"You know perfectly well that Miles Walsingham will not do."

"Because of the shallowness of his pockets, which, I am given to believe, he is fast rectifying? Now, you would saddle me with a nightmare for a mother-in-law? Besides, I do not find the Duke of Linborough's looks pleasing. He gives one the impression of being a very stubborn gentleman. I am sure I would not be happy, married to such a man." She gave her mother a heartrending look. "Do you not love me, Mama?"

Her mother frowned. "Please do not try my patience, Maude. My love for you has no bearing on the matter. Trust me darling, Her Grace presents no threat. With my guidance, you will soon have her claws pulled."

"Why should I have to go through all that, Mama? I do not wish to marry into such a family. Nothing you can say, will make me change my mind."

"You forget yourself, Maude. No gentleman will tolerate such behavior in a wife. Try to be more like Lucy. She is not given to such tantrums." She bestowed Lucy with a smile.

Lucy was dismayed. She knew it was an empty gesture. The lady was merely using her as a weapon against Maude. This was something new. She hoped Maude's mother did not intend to make a habit of using her in such a fashion, for she knew it could drive a wedge been Maude and her. The thought was unbearable. Maude's friendship meant too much to her.

"I am not so sure I want a husband." Maude replied. "Being married sounds very tiresome."

"If you are trying to upset me, give yourself a pat on the back, because you have succeeded. I do not know what has come over you, lately."

Her mother threw her head back and raised her hand to her brow. "What am I to do with you? Heaven knows I only have your best interests at heart. Left to your own devices, you would probably succumb to the charms of a penniless, younger son. One, no doubt, in possession of a glib tongue and a predilection for gaming."

Lucy detected sadness in her tone. She wondered if, perhaps when she was a girl, Lady Northwycke had been thwarted in a desire to marry such a person.

The dowager put her arm around Maude's shoulder. "Come now, darling, please be reasonable. I am only trying to do what is best for you." Her voice became honey-toned. "I am not suggesting you marry Robert Renquist, only, that should he decide to pay you court, you receive him graciously, as one would any eligible gentleman."

Maude looked relieved. "I am sure he is most amiable, once one gets beyond his stern demeanor."

"His stern demeanor?" Her mother's brows transformed into inverted vees. "Where do you get such odd notions? I think he is quite handsome, and found him to be most pleasant in his dealings with us."

"Really, Mama? How can you say that? Even you must see that his looks are most forbidding, and there is no true amiability to his nature. Look at the manner in which he used Lucy and me at Gunters—toying with us like a huge cat playing with two defenseless mice."

The dowager shook her head. "I fear you will have a difficult time in finding a husband, my daughter. The sort of paragon you seek does not exist, so I suggest you take a more realistic approach to choosing whom you will marry."

Maude gave an impatient shrug. "Mama. I am not a fool. I am well aware of that."

"Whether or not you are a fool, my child, is moot. Other young ladies have been setting their caps for the Duke of Linborough for several seasons, to no avail."

Maude smiled. "Perhaps His Grace is the one who seeks perfection. If he comes courting me, I fear, he is destined for disappointment, since, Mama, you have made it perfectly clear I am far from perfect."

The next morning, Maude and Lucy entered the drawing room and made their curtsies to the dowager. Lucy had been reluctant to be at the morning reception, but Maude had refused to attend without her. Lady Northwycke quizzed them with her lorgnette, as if looking for imperfections. It took all of Lucy's self-control not to squirm under her scrutiny.

"Charming, charming," the dowager enthused. "The new pink ribands are the perfect touch to your dress, Maude, dear. The ideal balance between innocence and budding young womanhood."

"Mama!" Maude flushed crimson.

Her mother laughed, and to Lucy's mortification, turned her attention to her. "I must say, the alterations to the yellow muslin, Maude outgrew, turned out rather well. The dress looks most becoming on you, Lucy."

Glowing with pleasure, Lucy curtsied. "Thank you, Madam, you are most kind."

She eyed Lucy once more. "I do believe you are putting on a little flesh. Perhaps there is hope for you yet, child."

Could that be? Lucy contemplated her bony wrists and decided her ladyship was deluded, or perhaps, merely trying to be kind. As far as she could determine, any change in her appearance, was, at best, infinitesimal.

The three of them had no sooner sat down, than the sound of horse's hooves clopping toward the house brought Maude to her feet.

"For goodness sake, Maude, do sit down. If you so much as even *look* as if you are going to the window, I declare I shall cancel your come-out next season. A lady should never appear to be eager."

Maude sounded aggrieved. "Eager? Really, Mama, for a moment I had thought to return to my bedchamber. I have no great inclination to see the Duke of Linborough. In fact, It would make no difference to me if he were never to grace one of our receptions."

Her mother towered over her. "I declare. You go out of your way to upset me. What do you want of me child?"

"Nothing. I just fail to see why it is so important for me to dance attendance on His Grace. Tell me, Mama, would he think I was biddable if I were to prostrate myself at his feet?"

Her mother tapped Maude's shoulder with her index finger. "I have had just about enough of your nonsense. I will thank you to sit down, and comport yourself as becomes the daughter of a marquess."

Maude complied, but not before rolling her eyes. "There is no cause for alarm," she said. "It was just a passing thought."

Lady Northwycke threw up her hands. "Maude, you are incorrigible. I shall deal with you later."

To Lucy's relief, the butler chose that moment to announce their first guest. "Mr. Miles Walsingham, my lady."

Lady Northwycke's face dropped. Maude giggled. As far as Lucy could see, matters were not improving, but at least, she was pleased that Miles had chosen to grace them with his presence. Maude and her mother would have to cease their bickering, and besides, the Marquess of Northwycke's brother-in-law, was a charming gentleman, who always treated her with the utmost consideration and cordiality.

Lady Northwycke as always, was the perfect hostess and her displeasure was not overt, but Lucy could tell by the tightness of the smile she directed towards Miles, that this particular morning, at least, his presence was not welcome.

Several people came and went in the first hour. Lucy wondered if her ladyship had been mistaken about the Duke of Linborough's intentions of paying them a visit. In which case, the uproar between Maude and her mother had been for naught.

Finally, the Duke of Linborough accompanied by his mother put in an appearance. It would seem that the Garwoods had been relegated to the last stop of their social round. Those present rose from their seats to bow and curtsey to the Renquists.

It did not take Lucy long to realize that Maude's mother was not the only one who did not welcome Miles Walsingham's company. This, she deduced from the Duchess of Linborough's apparent reaction to his presence. Her Grace did not give him the cut-direct, but whereas she greeted Lord and Lady Fotheringham most effusively, and seemed to play the coquette with James's old comrade-at-arms, Rodney Bonham-Lewis, Miles only merited a raised brow from the lady, accompanied by the merest vestige of a smile.

Almost immediately, Bonham-Lewis thanked his hostess for her hospitality, bowed to the assemblage, and took his leave, seemingly with more haste than dignity.

"How peculiar," said Lady Northwycke, wonderingly. "He did not even drink his tea."

Lucy found nothing peculiar in Rodney Bonham-Lewis, deeming the advantage of escaping the clutches of an amorous widow, preferable to dallying over a cup of tea, however nice it might be. However, she found it highly amusing that a man, who had fought Bonaparte's army at its worst, could find one small woman so intimidating.

The duchess gave his departing form a freezing glance, then sat down next to her hostess, her feathers all a ruffle. Lucy concluded that incurring the wrath of one so high in the instep as the Duchess of Linborough did not bode well for the gentleman's place in society.

Lucy noted that Her Grace's mood changed for the better, almost immediately. For her eyes gleamed with anticipation the moment that a footman brought over a tray of pastries, some filled with spiced meats, and others with fruits and rich cream concoctions.

"Would you care to partake of a little refreshment, Your Grace?" Lady Northwycke asked.

Her Grace brushed her hand across her stomach. "I should decline. But perhaps a little. Everything looks so delicious." She tittered, and pointed to the richest and creamiest of the confections for the footman to put on her plate, failing to stop him until the delicate Limoges porcelain was filled to capacity.

During the course of the following half-hour, Lucy was fascinated by the avidity with which the duchess ingested both food, *and* gossip. On the other hand, her son displayed no interest whatsoever in either, but leaned against the fireplace sipping tea, a distant look in his eyes.

Perhaps Maude is worrying for nothing, she thought. The duke seems not in the slightest bit interested in being here. For Maude's sake, I hope this is the case. He does not seem at all the sort of person that Maude should marry. Why can her mother not see that?

She took advantage of his pre-occupied state, to study him more closely. His face was such a paradox. Could one imagine a certain tenderness lurking behind those clear, blue eyes, and, perhaps, loneliness? How could this be? A powerful lord would not lack for friends. Perhaps the key to his character lies in his firm jaw, and deeply cleft chin. They bespoke an implacable nature.

She shivered at the thought of incurring the displeasure of such a personage, and yet she wondered what it was that pre-occupied his thoughts. It was obviously nothing or no one in the room…

To Lucy's horror, she realized the duke had caught her staring at him, for he was looking right at her, one eyebrow raised, a quizzical look on his face.

Lucy was paralyzed with shock at being caught in such brazen behavior, and did not, in fact could not lower her eyes right away, but continued to stare at the duke, who, in turn, stared right back.

She finally broke eye contact and turned her attention to her hands, which, as became a young lady of quality, were demurely folded in her lap. Convinced her behavior had brought shame upon herself; the heat of embarrassment flooded her cheeks. It was, as she feared, she was unfit to move in such exalted circles.

Robert Renquist had not come willingly to the house on Mayfair Court. He had no desire to further his acquaintance with the Garwood heiress. She seemed pleasant enough, and although she did not possess the pale, cameo beauty he favored when choosing a mistress, she had a certain classic elegance—but what on earth would they share in common? Good Heavens, she had only recently celebrated her sixteenth birthday! He was ten years her senior and after helping rout Napoleon from the Spanish Peninsula, felt considerably older.

He watched his mother nibble at her third pastry, the crumbs catching in the lace at her bodice, and realized she was beginning to develop a second chin. She had always been celebrated for her great beauty—when had she become just another aging matron? he wondered. Perhaps only yesterday, for he had not noticed the transformation.

Saddened by the idea, he averted his eyes. It was the first time he had ever thought of his mother in terms of growing old, and the consequences of such, sent a shiver down his spine. It will devastate her, he thought. I know her constant demands can be exasperating, but she is my mother and I love her. Do not most great beauties rely on their faces to get what they want? I should know. I have succumbed to enough of their wiles in my time.

He glanced across the room. Lady Maude was engaged in an earnest conversation with Miles Walsingham, a young man of fine bloodlines, but of no consequence, according to his mother, merely to be tolerated because of his connection by marriage to the Garwoods. It occurred to Robert, that his mother assessed people rather in the manner a horse-fancier, evaluates the contents of his stable.

The wraith-like Miss Garwood sat next to Lady Maude. His eyes wandered no farther. The bold creature was studying his face in a most penetrating manner. He raised a brow to stare her down. This tactic usually intimidated the most brazen of people, but to his surprise, seemingly absorbed by his face, she did not break eye contact right away. He found her behavior positively unnerving.

By Jove, he thought, I do believe that the impudent little Bath miss is trying to stare *me* down. Better than she, have tried and failed. Good heavens, the girl does not even blink. Robert was beginning to wonder if she would ever back down. I wish I had ignored her, he thought, she is beginning to make me feel deucedly uncomfortable. Lord, is she actually going to win this silly battle of wills?

To his relief, she finally lowered her gaze. He took satisfaction in the pink glow he perceived to be coloring her cheeks. Good, he thought, she has the grace to blush. The odd creature has earned her discomfort. Such an attitude in one so young. How old could she be? Fourteen? Fifteen, at most.

I have never met a girl quite like her. She boldly confronted me at Gunter's yesterday afternoon, and today, almost succeeds in staring me down in a most unmaidenly fashion. Probably the result of cousins marrying cousins, an aberration for which those Shrewsbury Garwoods are notorious.

Deciding he could put off his social obligations no longer, he placed his cup and saucer on the mantel and joined the young trio. Lady Maude gave him a welcoming smile. Miles Walsingham, swiftly rose, almost knocking over the delicate Chippendale chair he occupied, in his haste to bow to him. Miss Garwood accorded him the weakest of smiles, then swiftly resumed staring at her lap. He presumed there would be no conversation from *that* quarter, unless he solicited it.

"Do pull up a chair, Your Grace," Maude said.

Robot complied, taking a chair, which matched Miles Walsingham's. It occurred to him that both of them looked somewhat ridiculous perched on the flimsy pieces.

"We were discussing Hope House, Your Grace." Miles offered this information with an ingratiating smile.

Robert did not smile back. Naturally, he was used to, and expected the deference due his rank, but he detested those who fawned over him as a means to curry favor.

"Hope House?" he replied. "I am afraid you have the advantage of me, sir. I have never heard of it."

Maude answered for Miles. "It is an asylum for children, my brother and his wife have founded."

"Really? There is a need for such, at Northwycke? I have found that in most cases, country families are close-knit and at

Linborough, apart from the occasional basket delivered by my mother and sisters, the cottagers take care of their own."

"Out of the forty or so children residing at Hope House, only one, an infant named William, comes from the village," Maude explained. "The rest are rescued from the very worst parts of this city. Children who otherwise would be condemned to lives of utter degradation."

To his surprise, Miss Garwood sprang to life, and jumped into the discussion. "For instance, the latest acquisition is a little chimney-sweep named Tim, who will probably never regain the use of his left arm. It was injured while being dragged from a chimney flue. It is feared his arm will wither. One would think there would be an alternative way of getting get rid of soot, other than endangering the lives and health of small boys. Our society has a great deal for which to answer."

"Quite," Robert replied. "But would it not have been better to let the little wretch die? What sort of life does he have to look forward to, with such a handicap?"

"Better to let him die?" Lucy half rose from her seat.

Robert was taken aback. Her eyes blazing with indignation, the mouse had become a tigress.

Lucy slumped back into her seat. "Thank heavens, Cousin James does not follow that sort of reasoning. I agree letting him die is by far, the simpler solution. After all, to those of privilege, what does it matter, one way or the other, how many slum children die?"

Robert had never been treated so cavalierly in his life, yet he was intrigued by the turn the conversation had taken. Of a certainty, it was not one's average drawing room fare. "I have a feeling you are about to tell me, Miss Garwood."

"That is simple, Your Grace, most members of the *ton* do not give such matters a second thought."

The tension between the four, crackled. Maude leaned forward, her lips parted, as if in anticipation of further excitement Robert was tempted to kiss her, then realized where he was.

Miles, on the other hand, looked mortified, but surely

not for himself? Had he a *tendre* for Miss Garwood, perhaps? Impossible. The man had to be a fortune hunter. Robert came to the conclusion that the chit was in possession of a considerable fortune to gain such attention. It occurred to him that Mr. Walsingham had better be in possession of considerable patience, it would be quite a while before the girl would be of an age to marry.

His train of thought was interrupted by the sound of his mother's's voice drifting across the room. "But of course," she was saying, "one has to put those dreadful mushrooms in their place, or before you know it, they have our daughters running off to Gretna Green. Anything to gain entree into polite society. I understand such was the case with that dreadful Smythe-Jones."

"You were saying, Miss Garwood?" Robert inserted, not wishing to hear any more of his mother's vapid words.

"Are you sure you wish to continue this conversation, Your Grace? I feel I should apologize for my outburst. When I think of all the cruelties that are inflicted upon innocent children, I sometimes forget myself"

Nevertheless, Robert noted, however much Miss Garwood might feel an apology was necessary, she did not actually deliver one. Perhaps the young lady should not be let off too lightly.

"Nonsense." Robert dismissed her transgressions with an expansive smile—the sort he saved for an enemy on the battlefield, before delivering the *coup-de-grace*. "Pray continue."

She inclined her head. More of a nervous bob, than a nod. "If it is your wish, sir. It is necessary to point out that young Tim's arm, or lack, thereof, has no bearing on the outcome of his future."

Robert raised a brow. It was time to poke a few holes in the young girl's theories. "Surely the Marquess does not intend to keep him in idleness for the rest of his life? What sort of existence would that be?"

"Sir, I did not mean to imply that the boy was destined for a life of sloth, nor would I wish such, upon him. In the short time he has been at Hope House, it has been ascertained that he is in possession of a keen intelligence. Not only has he grasped the rudiments of reading, and penmanship, but also shows an aptitude for figures. When he is of an age, Cousin James intends to put his talents to use in his maritime affairs."

It was clear to Robert that this was a subject very dear to Miss Garwood's heart. Her delivery rang with sincerity and as her passion soared, her face took on a rosy glow. He found this to be fascinating. For a brief moment, the girl looked almost pretty.

"It is most surprising," Maude inserted, "several of the children seem to be quite bright."

Robert resigned himself to the fact there would be no victory for him today, and ceased to be combative. "You have seen this for yourself, Lady Maude?"

She gave a deprecating little shrug. "Alas, I have visited the home but once. My mother forbids it."

"I am not surprised."

Maude grinned. "She is afraid I might catch something nasty from the children. But my brother's wife could be found there every day, playing with the babies. That is, until she became er-with child, herself. Then my brother suggested that she also should stay away."

"One could hardly blame him. So right now, you have no real contact with this place?"

"Lucy—that is—Miss Garwood, goes over most days— weather permitting."

Robert could not think of a less appropriate name for such an unprepossessing female. Lucinda, probably her real name, evoked a vision of breathless beauty. His third mistress, to be precise. A raven-haired, violet-eyed, young widow of an elderly viscount. She had left him for a gentleman who had offered her marriage to assure her favors. Something, Robert had not been willing to do. His duchess had to be above reproach.

"She is worth her weight in gold."

"Hmm?" For a moment. Robert thought Lady Maude was reading his thoughts.

"My cousin, Miss Garwood. She not only teaches those children their lessons, she also helps care for the babies in my sister-in-law's stead."

"Do you not have nursemaids for this task?"

"Of course, Your Grace," Maude said. "It is all they can do to keep the little ones clean and fed. This is not enough. Babies need to be kissed and cuddled and sung to. This need is filled by this dear, sweet girl." Maude gave Lucy's hand an affectionate squeeze.

Robert was perplexed. "At your age, Miss Garwood, should you not be attending to your own lessons?"

"That was my brother's thought," Maude said, "but when my governess attempted to instruct Lucy—Miss Garwood—it was ascertained that she was far ahead of the governess in most subjects, including Latin and Greek. My brother was astounded by her erudition."

Robert gave Miss Garwood a pitying look. He hoped for her sake, that she had a king's ransom for a dowry, for in truth, it seemed she had nothing else in her favor.

When Robert and his mother departed for home, he decided that neither of the Garwood girls were to his liking. Not that Miss Lucy Garwood was even of an age to be considered. Granted, he had been tempted to plant a kiss on Lady Maude's rosy lips, but he was between mistresses, and attributed this urge to unmet needs.

All the same, rather than incur his mother's lamentations, he decided that next season, he would go through the motions of courting Lady Maude, taking good care that another of her suitors proposed to her first. There were ways of making sure one did not present oneself as *too* endearing!

Four

Lucy was thrilled with her new clothes. Whenever alone she preened in front of her bedroom mirror to admire the fine tucks and laces of the dress she had on. She was not a vain girl, her own features received scant attention during this process, but she had watched her mother sew for long hours, creating garments for ladies of quality, and she had grown to appreciate their beauty. Not in the wildest flights of fancy had she envisioned owning such beautiful things.

In the expectation that good food would add flesh to Lucy's meager form, the older Lady Northwycke had wisely instructed the mantuamaker to put ample seams in her clothes. By March, they had to be let out. Lucy applied herself to this task, taking care to resew the garments with tiny, even stitches

Lady Northwycke studied Lucy's handiwork with her lorgnette. "You have been taught well, Lucy. Your needlework puts that of Mrs. Eliot's girls to shame."

Lucy flushed with pleasure. "Thank you, madam. I would be glad to take care of any mending you might have."

The dowager nodded. "Yes. I rather expect you would. You are a most obliging young lady, but it is enough that you take care of your own clothes." She scrutinized Lucy's figure. "I would suggest that you try not to get any fatter, dear. Your figure has attained certain elegance. It would be a pity to lose it before you find a husband."

Lucy was too embarrassed to offer a reply. Her own mother had been modest to a fault. Lucy doubted she would ever get used to Lady Northwycke's outspoken manner. Besides, did she not have at least two more years before she had to think about marriage?

She was greatly relieved when James's wife, the younger Lady Northwycke, entered the room before the subject could be pursued any further. Emily was in the sixth month of her pregnancy. Her bouts of early-morning sickness being a thing of the past, she glowed with the happiness of expectant motherhood. She had recently celebrated her eighteenth birthday, and with her lustrous black hair and rose petal complexion, Lucy thought she looked like a princess of ancient legend.

Emily bade them both good morning, then addressed Lucy. "Monsieur Voudray awaits you in the music room. You will be practicing the waltz, I believe."

Lucy raised a brow. "I had thought with Maude being indisposed the lesson would be postponed."

"Not at all," Emily replied. "It will afford you the opportunity to refine your skills. I shall provide the music."

The older Lady Northwycke rose. "I should like to see how you are coming along."

The dancing master and Lucy traversed the parquet floor only once, when the dowager ceased beating time to the lilting tune to whisper to her daughter-in-law, "I think you should watch this. Tell me, Emily, am I not correct in thinking a lady should not dance in such a fashion?"

Emily glanced toward Lucy and shrugged. "I see nothing untoward, Mother. She is as graceful as any dancer at the opera."

"But that is the *point* I am trying to make, dear. Ought a lady to arch her neck and back in such a fashion? I suppose this comes of having a common dancing girl for a grandmother."

"Do not give it another thought, Mother. I think Lucy is destined to be the belle of the ball in another year or two."

Emily's mother-in-law shook her head. "For goodness' sake, do not put any ideas of that nature in the child's head. I am afraid that Lucy will not be attending any balls. With her doubtful parentage she can scarcely be thrust upon an unsuspecting society, at least not until she is safely married to some respectable country squire."

Emily stopped playing. "Then is it not cruel to teach her such graces?"

"Not at all. It is doubtful she will associate with those of the blood-royal, but she is bound to attend dances within her own shire. Squires do attend such functions. Heaven knows I have had my feet trampled on by those worthies enough times. It is the curse of belonging to the leading family of a parish."

"You are right, of course. But it seems so cruel for the poor girl to observe Maude enjoying the delights of a come-out that she herself will be denied."

"Do not dwell on it, Emily. None of us gets our every wish fulfilled. Lucy has been more fortunate than she ever had a right to expect. I am sure the girl gets down on her knees to give thanks every time she prepares for bed."

Before Emily could reply, Lucy came over to the piano. "Oh dear. Is anything the matter? I expect I need to practice my steps a little better."

Emily gave her a reassuring smile. "Not at all. I have never seen anyone dance the waltz with quite such grace and charm." She nodded to the dancing master. "You may take the rest of the afternoon off, sir. You have taught Miss Garwood well."

Monsieur Voudray executed the most elegant of bows. "Alas, it would not become me to take zee credit for Mees Garwood's dancing. The young lady 'as an inborn talent. The muse, Terpsichore, was most generous, I am thinking."

"Quite so." Nevertheless, the older Lady Northwycke did not look pleased. "It is time for me to give Maude some more of that dreadful elixir Dr. Mainwaring left for her." She wrinkled her nose. "I rather suspect by its foul odor it consists of eye of newt and tail of something or other, however that incantation goes. One cannot be expected to remember every word Mr. Shakespeare saw fit to put on paper."

Emily nodded in agreement. "It is unfortunate Maude got caught in the rain. The weather is so capricious this time of year."

The Frenchman rolled his eyes. "*Madame*, it ees not unreasonable to say that zee English weather is unpredictable at all times of zee year. My 'ome was in zee south of France, and there are times I theenk I shall never be warm again." He bowed to each of the ladies in turn and departed the room.

"How odd," the dowager said. "What a talkative fellow. Monsieur Voudray forgets his place, would you not agree? Where on earth did James find him?"

Emily shrugged. "I really could not say, Mother, but he came with the most impeccable references, and as James said, he is far too old to make amorous advances toward his charges." She stood and rubbed the small of her back.

The older woman eyed the gesture. "You had better put your feet up, child. You must not strain yourself in your delicate condition."

Emily did not argue the point. "Some days my back bothers me more than others. I had no idea I would get so big. No wonder ladies go into hiding at such times."

"As well they should." The dowager sniffed. "I have no patience with creatures who flaunt their condition in public places, with absolutely no consideration for the sensibilities of others."

After the older Lady Northwycke had departed for her own house, Lucy walked Emily to her room. Jealous of her position, Emily's abigail lost no time in elbowing Lucy out of the way. As Lucy walked to her own chamber, she could hear Susan fuss and cluck like a mother hen as she helped Emily out of her clothes.

She picked up some sewing, but could not concentrate on repairing the delicate lace that had come undone on her petticoat. She put it aside in favor of taking a stroll in the gardens. Lucy always felt at her happiest where she could be among the trees and grass and smell the sweet perfume of the flowers.

When she came to the fork in the path, she was reminded it was time to pay Mickey Dempsey a visit. She knew Mickey loved working in the stables. He treated every horse entrusted to his care like a precious child. It was also a great relief to Lucy to know he had fulfilled a long-held dream of having a cottage in the country where he could grow flowers and vegetables. But Lucy suspected that there were times he felt lonely away from his cronies and the bustle of city life, so she made the time to visit him, when possible.

She headed to the stables and arrived in time to catch Mickey giving the final stroke of a brush to a horse he had just washed. A bay gelding, brother to James's horse, Tarquin. On seeing Lucy, he led the horse into the paddock and with a friendly slap to his rump set him off to a brisk trot.

Lucy leaned on the paddock fence. "He is a handsome horse, but he lacks Tarquin's spirit, would you not agree?"

"He wouldn't have, would he? Being a gelding, an' all."

"Oh, I was not aware."

"No reason why you should be, is there, Miss Lucy?"

"No, I suppose not. I just thought I would see how you were. It's a nice day for a walk."

"I suppose."

"Tell me, Mickey, are you glad you came here?"

"Of course I am, girl. London is a cesspool."

"You are not too lonely here?"

Mickey grinned, revealing that he was missing most of his front teeth. "You've heard something then?"

Lucy had known him too long. It was obvious he had a secret he was dying to share. "No, Mickey. But if there is something, I prefer to hear it from you."

"I'm glad you came by, you'd've found out on Sunday, in any case."

"Found out what?"

"That I am going to get wed. The parson'll be reading the banns, starting next Sunday."

Lucy beamed. "Really? I think that is marvelous. Do I know the bride?"

"Maggie Purdy."

"One of the dairymaids? Congratulations, Mickey. And here I was worrying you might be lonely."

Mickey kicked the dirt with his boot. "Maggie may not be well-favored, but when you look at my ugly mug, I consider myself lucky she'll 'ave me. She 'as a kind 'eart, and that's the main thing."

"It is not only the main thing, Mickey, it is everything. I never thought you would do it. You were always so set against getting married."

"That was in London. I would've never run the risk of bringing kiddies into the world in that hellhole. But Northwycke is a nice little place."

"Does his lordship know?"

"Of course. Told 'im yesterday, right after I talked to the parson."

"He did not mention it." Lucy felt slighted.

"'E wouldn't, would 'e? Wasn't 'is secret to tell."

"Of course. How silly of me. If the banns are going to be read and everything, I suppose you will not mind if I tell Lady Maude?"

"Not at all. She's always treated me well. I'm glad you 'ave her for a friend. Sort of sets my mind at ease."

Lucy laughed. "What a coincidence. I thought the very same thing about you when you said you were marrying Maggie."

James Elias came into the world on the first day in June, roaring his indignation over the treatment he had received on the journey. He was a rosy baby with a crown of dark curls, who after an initial bout of colic, proved to be a sunny-natured child. Everyone, from the lowliest nursemaid to his lordship, vied to see who could spoil him the most.

When it was Lucy's turn to hold him, she would nuzzle his neck and drink in the sweetness of his perfume. It had been her experience that babies were damp little creatures, prone to reek of sour milk—or worse. From the first time she held her baby cousin close to her, she felt an overwhelming tenderness for the child. It took no time at all for the emotion to deepen into love.

Strangely enough, her attachment to the baby boy made her even more aware of her status as an outsider in the Garwood household. Emily and James would take him to their own chambers. The sound of their laughter mingling with the delighted gurgles of their son made Lucy acutely aware they were part of a magic circle, and despite the kindness shown her, she could never be included.

It was not until Emily's brother finally came to Northwycke Hall toward the end of July to see his nephew for the first time that Lucy discovered she was not the only one beset by a sense of apartness.

The day after Miles arrived proved to be a glorious day. The sun dappled the English countryside, and there was not the slightest threat of a pending thunderstorm making it the perfect day for a picnic by the lake.

Being a spur-of-the-moment decision, no one outside of the family was asked to attend. The table linen was spread on the grass, and the participants sat on blankets and cushions.

While they partook of a substantial meal of savory pies, roasted pheasant, and an assortment of fruits and vegetables, complemented by jugs of milk and decanters of the sauterne, to which James was partial, James Elias slept peacefully in a wicker basket, under the shade of a horse chestnut tree. As if on cue, the moment the remains of the picnic were cleared away, he stirred, and started to fuss.

The nursemaid who danced attendance changed his clothes, then handed him over to Emily. Maude and Lucy joined her, each waiting their turn to hold him. Emily waved them away. "You will both have to wait. James and I wish to introduce our son to the wonder of nature. Is that not so, darling?"

James rose, and brushed the crumbs from his well-fitting trousers. "I believe that was the agreement."

Lucy took great pride in being related to such a well-favored man. With a pang of sorrow, she realized that is how her own dear father would have looked had he not suffered a life of deprivation.

The baby's grandmother rose and shook out the rumpled skirt of her muslin gown. "What possible advantage could there be to that, pray tell? The child is scarcely two months old."

It seemed that James was not about to have his good spirits dampened by his mother's negative attitude, and with an indulgent laugh he replied, "One is never too young to inhale the perfume of the meadow flowers. A rose is no sweeter than the primrose or the honeysuckle."

His mother gave him a look.

James took the baby from Emily, and the trio took off across the meadow, the lively chatter of the married couple rivaling the birdsong.

"I declare," the dowager said to no one in particular. "I rather suspect my son is completely addled. Whoever heard of a man paying such close attention to a child who is not even into short coats?"

Miles joined Maude and Lucy, who were still standing under the horse chestnut tree, watching James and Emily's progress through the grass. "Would you two young ladies care to join me for a walk around the lake?"

Maude looked askance. "Surely you do not intend to walk all the way around in this heat?"

"Not quite. The lakeshore has enough trees to offer shade, but to be perfectly honest, I was merely considering a short stroll to help walk off that large luncheon."

Lucy said, "Let me get my parasol. I would be delighted to accompany you."

"Capital," Miles rejoined.

"You two enjoy your walk," Maude said. "If you do not mind, I prefer to sit under this tree. It is beastly hot."

Miles and Lucy walked the first few hundred yards in complete silence. They came upon a bench beneath the trees, and Miles gestured toward it. Lucy sat down.

Neither one spoke. The silence weighed on Lucy like a pall, and she frantically searched her mind for something to say—anything at all, but words eluded her. She watched a duck glide across the lake, a string of ducklings in tow, then she gave her full attention to a dragonfly skimming the water's surface in quest of prey. She was about to make an inane remark regarding the beauty of nature when Miles initiated a conversation.

"I could not help but notice the expression on your face when James and Emily departed with their son. You must learn not to expose your feelings to public scrutiny."

Lucy felt a heat that had nothing to do with the weather. "I—I am sure I do not know what you mean."

"Of course you do, dear girl. Those thoughts must haunt your every waking hour."

"Please, Miles, I have no idea what you are talking about. Why are you being so horrid? I thought you were my friend."

He took her hand. It was a liberty completely alien to Lucy, and she quickly withdrew it from his clasp.

"My apologies, Lucy. In my clumsy fashion I am trying to tell you that I recognize your loneliness in the midst of other people's happiness."

Lucy was dismayed. Was she so transparent? "H—how could you possibly know the way I feel?"

"Because, Lucy, those feelings echo mine."

"Please, do not make sport of me, Miles. Your ties to this family and acceptance in society are not tainted with subterfuge."

"Are they not? Through my own stupidity I almost ruined my sister's life, and to this day would not be received by people of discernment were it not for my connections to your uncle. No. I, too, am denied entry to the banquet and must be content to watch on the side while others partake of the feast."

"Oh, Miles, you *do* understand. You have no idea how guilty I feel at times for harboring such ignoble thoughts. I have been treated so kindly I sometimes pinch myself to make sure I am not dreaming. It is just that somewhere in this world I like to think there might be a place that is meant for me."

Miles patted her hand. "I am sure there must be. Who knows? Perhaps one day you and I shall partake of our own banquet." He laughed, as if to lighten his words. Lucy joined in. It was nice of Miles to want to cheer her up.

Later that night, as she lay in her bed, watching the moonlight stream through the window, his words echoed in her mind. She sighed. It was unfortunate they were spoken in jest. Perhaps sharing life's banquet with someone as charming as Miles would be a very pleasant experience.

Five

Summer passed and Maude spent the winter months preparing for her entry into society the following spring. The long awaited London Season of 1815 arrived, and young people of both sexes, hoping to attract the love of someone amiable, good to look upon, and above all, in possession of a handsome fortune, eagerly hied to the City.

The Garwoods celebrated Easter at the parish church, St. Cuthbert's, followed by a feast at Northwycke Hall, and the following Tuesday the whole family, including Lucy, departed for the house in Mayfair. Even though Lucy had celebrated two joint birthdays with Maude, and as many Christmases, she was still awed by the lavish amount of food and drink the *ton* deemed such occasions called for.

Every person of consequence had been invited to the ball the Marquess of Northwycke was hosting to honor the come-out of his seventeen-year old sister, and few had declined. It promised to be the most lavish affair of the Season.

When the evening of Maude's ball finally arrived, she presented herself for Lucy's inspection. "Will I do?" she asked, her forehead wrinkled with doubt.

Would she do? In a gown of white with an overtunic of soft green sarcenet, its tiny puff sleeves dimpled with sprigs of pristine white silk snowdrops, Maude had never looked lovelier.

"You look splendid, Maude, dear. Absolutely splendid."

Maude's frown was replaced with a beaming smile. "That is such a relief to hear you say. You know so much about female attire. Your suggestion of trimming the green with the snowdrops was the crowning touch."

Lucy shrugged. "It was nothing. They happened to catch

my eye among the assortment Mrs. Eliot had on hand."

"I feel absolutely horrid about you not attending the ball. It will not be the same without you."

Lucy had mixed feelings about being left out of the festivities. "I do not wish you to take offense at my words, Maude, but I find the thought of attending such an affair to be most daunting."

"I hope you outgrow your aversion. I am sure balls are most jolly."

Lucy shrugged. "You must forgive me if I do not agree."

Maude's eyes widened. "How could one *not* wish to attend?"

Lucy marveled at her self-confidence. "How?" she countered. The Duke of Linborough had been right in his assessment of the Lady Maude; life held no fears for her. "Suppose the most wonderful young man, I mean *the* one in the whole wide world with whom you would like to spend the rest of your life, just suppose he asks you to dance?"

Maude executed a pirouette, her arms outstretched. "Would that not be wonderful?"

"No."

"No?"

"Not if you tread on his feet while dancing, or spill your punch over his beautifully embroidered waistcoat. Just picture the consequences of either mishap. This paragon of manhood would be sure to bow, take his leave, nevermore to seek your company."

"Oh dear," Maude replied. "I do so wish you had not put such a thought in my head." She caught a twinkle in Lucy's eye and burst out laughing. "You little villain, you were teasing me."

Lucy hugged her. "I had to do something to make light of the moment. Have a wonderful time at your ball, and tell me all about it tomorrow. I am just happy for not being left behind at Northwycke Hall."

"Our darling Emily is the one who suggested you be allowed to come with us."

"Emily. Of course. She has a knack for putting herself in the place of others."

"Mama says it is because of the trying time she had before

marrying my brother."

"Trying time?"

Maude placed a finger to her lips. *"Big* family secret. Perhaps one day Emily will tell you all about it."

Lucy could think of nothing more marvelous than to be taken into Emily's confidence, but she doubted it would happen.

When Maude joined the rest of the family in the ballroom to await the arrival of their guests, she left a lingering trace of lavender in her wake. Lucy inhaled the perfume; it gave her a feeling of well-being. She picked up a camisole lying on the thick blue and gold carpet, folded it, placed it on a dresser of burled walnut, and with one final glance around the cosy room left for her own bedchamber.

Robert Renquist loathed London. He especially loathed it during the time termed the Season, for then the city teamed with ambitious mamas with daughters to marry off. They seemed to scurry about everywhere, like ants departing a disturbed hill, for no matter how hard he tried to avoid them, he would be cornered at every turn and forced to suffer an introduction to one simpering Bath miss after another.

The sound of the longcase clock in the reception hall, chiming 11 P.M., accompanied by the equally noisy rustle of taffeta, heralded the entry into the room of his mother, and his sisters, Esther and Miriam.

The pale blue watered silk gown with its overlay of silver tissue looked most becoming on his mother, and he told her so, and followed the compliment with a filial peck to her cheek. She responded with a graceful curtsy, then directed his attention to his sisters with a gesture of a fan fashioned of osprey feathers.

He loved them both, but no matter how magnificently gowned they might be, they could never be considered beautiful. Esther had inherited their mother's blond coloring, but her small, doll-like features looked incongruous on her six-foot frame. The profusion of ringlets with which she dressed her hair, and the frilly pink dress she wore, did nothing to rectify her shortcomings.

Miriam, on the other hand, had inherited the duchess's small stature, the late duke's sparse brown hair, and, alas, his square jaw. This attribute might have endowed a long line of Renquist males with a certain air of masculine strength and virility, but not so poor Miriam. The dress of yellow satin she had chosen to wear for the evening compounded her lack of beauty by overpowering her pale complexion.

Robert bowed to each of his sisters. "You are both in extremely high feather this evening, my compliments on your lovely attire."

Esther simpered like an overgrown schoolgirl. "We have Mama to thank for that."

Robert felt the stirrings of resentment toward his mother. She knew exactly what to wear to enhance her own beauty, why could she not do the same for Esther and Miriam? Was it possible that she deliberately went out of her way to make them look that bad? He dismissed this thought as ignoble. His first judgment had been correct. Nothing could enhance a beauty that did not exist.

Robert's worst fears were confirmed. Northwycke's ball was a sad crush, in other words, with everyone of consequence in attendance; it would probably be considered the most successful event of the Season. The sort of affair he absolutely detested.

After making sure the ladies of his family were comfortably seated, he dutifully promised the requisite dances. This being accomplished, he scanned the ballroom for Lady Maude. He would dance with the girl but once, otherwise his mother would never let him hear the end of the matter.

In truth, Robert wished to marry for love, but so far the emotion had eluded him. He wondered why young girls had to be such prattling bores, and even worse, why sooner or later, he probably would have no recourse other than to marry one of them. His jaw stiffened. It would not be this Season.

Having recently parted with a mistress who had developed a regrettable penchant for young men in uniform, he seized the opportunity to seek out more seasoned beauties. Robert frowned on the custom of pursuing other men's wives, no matter how willing, but he deemed the occasional bedding of a comely young widow an act of mutual benefit.

The dancers swayed to the strains of a waltz. The movement of gauzy dresses afforded tantalizing glimpses of feminine charms. More than one adventurous beauty tossed him an alluring smile over the shoulder of an unsuspecting husband. "Egad," he muttered under his breath. "The little jades hawk their charms rather in the manner of costermongers vending fruit on street corners."

He caught his breath as a vision in pale green came into view. She was tall for a female. Two inches under six feet, he estimated. Her bosom was high and well rounded, and her hips short, most of her height stemming from deliciously long legs. Exactly the sort of woman who would fit well with his six-foot-two frame. He watched her progress around the room with admiration. She held her head high, like a proud swan, and her glorious auburn curls danced with fire.

Auburn hair? He favored beauties with raven tresses and milk white skin, but he had to admit the girl in the green dress had the figure and bearing of a goddess. Under the circumstances he was perfectly willing to widen his preferences as to her color. He waited for her to circle the ballroom once more, eager to get a clear view of her face. *No doubt that will prove to be an antidote*, he thought gloomily.

When the dancer finally came within his orbit, he viewed her straight Grecian nose and eyes sparkling amber fire and he let out a groan. How could Maude Garwood have transformed from a schoolgirl into this magnificent creature in less than a year?

Overwhelming desire took Robert by surprise. Embarrassed and confused, he turned heel and sought the refuge of an outside balcony. He leaned over the columned balustrade and breathed in the crisp, spring air. Perhaps it would cool the fever coursing through his blood. As he pondered his plight, the merry lilt of a quadrille filled the air.

He mopped his brow. His present condition precluded any participation in the festivities. He wondered at his lack of self-control. It was all so futile. There was only one way he could take Lady Maude to bed, and he was not yet ready to be leg-shackled—was he? Absolutely not!

As if to mock him, the muffled laughter of a man and a woman rose from the garden below. He decided that the sooner he acquired a new mistress, the better. Harboring lascivious thoughts about innocent maidens went beyond the pale.

The couple laughed once more. It was the slap and tickle sort of gaiety that bespoke a lighthearted dalliance rather than a grand passion. He peered over the balustrade to see who they were, but the dark of the night obscured the lovers from view. He wondered how the man had been able to convince the female to toss her petticoats on such a bone-chilling night.

His own ardor somewhat cooled, he returned to the ballroom just in time to espy Viscount Langley, the oldest son of the Earl of Larchville, returning Lady Maude to her seat beside her mother. At four-and-twenty the viscount was three years his junior, therefore of an age to be married and of sufficient fortune to be an eligible match for the Garwood girl.

Hope rose in Robert's breast. Perhaps Langley would win her heart, thereby allowing him yet another year for love to come his way.

The viscount leaned over and whispered something in Lady Maude's ear. She responded with a laugh. A low-pitched sound. Musical. Fraught with merriment Robert realized he was being irrational, but he was irked by the younger man's easy ability to amuse the girl.

It seemed to Robert that the young puppy was deliberately prolonging his leave-taking of the comely Maude. Robert was taken aback. At what point had he ceased to think of her in terms of her honorific in favor of the more intimate first-name basis?

Finally, Viscount Langley bowed to the older Lady Northwycke, then to her daughter, Lady Maude, and took his leave. Robert came forward, barely beating a pimple-faced youth to her presence. It suddenly occurred to him that it was so late in the evening that Lady Maude had most likely promised all her dances to others.

"I have an opening right after the very next dance, Your Grace." She smiled, then added, "That is, if it pleases you. A waltz, I believe."

"It pleases me very much, Lady Maude." After exchanging a few pleasantries, he bowed and took his leave, surprised that a waltz of all things was still available. The goddess in green was clearly the most beautiful girl in the room. Little did he know that her mother had shrewdly seen to it that a couple of choice dances had been kept available for such an eventuality.

In the meantime, he fulfilled the obligation of dancing the cotillion with his mother. She took his arm, a satisfied look on her face. "I saw you requesting a dance with Lady Maude. I trust you will diligently pursue this matter. I am tired of you allowing the most suitable girls of the Season to go to lesser men year after year."

"For pity's sake, Mother, pray let us postpone this conversation until we are within the privacy of our own house. I do not relish the idea of being discussed in every drawing room in London."

Before she could respond, they were absorbed into a group of eight, and participating in the dance. Robert knew it was but a brief respite, and his mother would continue the onerous conversation at the earliest possible convenience.

When it came time to dance the waltz with Lady Maude, Robert squired her around the floor twice before initiating a conversation.

"My compliments, Lady Maude. You look most charming this evening. Such a becoming shade of green."

Maude beamed. There was no upswept glance, or the flutter of eyelashes that a compliment usually evoked. "Yes, is it not? When Mama picked out the material, I thought it to be most odious. I should have known better. She is very clever about such things."

Robert smiled. Lady Maude may look like a goddess, he thought, but she is still a schoolgirl. Open, bubbly, and completely without guile. He doubted it was even in her to conduct a harmless flirtation, much less rise to the heights of passion. He fought the urge to smile. The thought of awakening ardor in the bosom of innocence filled him with a certain wicked pleasure.

He saw a questioning look appear in her eyes, and guilt over harboring such scandalous thoughts about an innocent girl caused him to wonder if she had read his mind. He dismissed this notion as being too fanciful. *She is probably wondering what I find so amusing,* he decided.

They spoke very little after that. In truth, Robert received more pleasure in holding her in his arms and drinking in her perfume than in any conversation she had to offer. In this, she was no different from any other young girl whose company he had been forced to suffer. So he wondered what perverse part of his nature induced him to ask her for another dance.

As it happened, Lady Maude did have a dance unclaimed, a quadrille, two dances hence. He would have preferred the intimacy of another waltz, but realized he had only himself to blame that none were available. He returned Lady Maude to her seat, then sought out his sister, Miriam, to claim the quadrille he had promised her.

He had thought earlier on that he might ask a young widow of his acquaintance for a dance—a vivacious young woman named Isobel, who was about three years his junior, with cat green eyes and saucy black curls. Since the war with Napoleon, it seemed that comely young widows were as plentiful as apples in an orchard.

Their paths had crossed at various functions, but so far he had confined his pursuit of her to flirtatious exchanges. As far as he was concerned, she had to carry the dalliance to the next level. He was not inclined to take advantage of anyone vulnerable. Especially the widow of a fellow officer.

He resolved to request a dance from the lady as soon as he had fulfilled his obligation to his sister. While waiting for the music to start, he espied Lady Maude in the adjoining set of eight. Her partner was Viscount Langley. *Good*, he thought. *I doubt it will take her too long to gaffe that impressionable young fish. He looks to be an easy catch.*

The next dance was a waltz. He espied Isobel standing in a

comer by herself, languidly waving her fan. The deep blue dress she wore suited her very well. Her husband had been killed early on in the war, so she had been out of mourning for quite some time.

Robert was halfway to her when Rodney Bonham-Lewis popped out of nowhere and claimed her first. He watched them converse on the ballroom floor while waiting for the music to start. They seemed to be on very friendly terms. Then he remembered Isobel had followed the drum, and Rodney had been in the same regiment as her husband.

He stepped back into the shadows and watched the couples swirling to the music. He caught a glimpse of Lady Maude's green dress from across the room but could not identify her partner.

Then he espied Isobel and Rodney Bonham-Lewis circling to the left of the ballroom. He saw Bonham-Lewis whisper in her ear, and she whispered back. When they reached the window to the terrace, they cut out of the dance and disappeared outside. *So much for considering the sensibilities of the gentler sex*, Robert thought.

When it was time to claim his dance with Lady Maude, she seemed as fresh and as energetic as the first time he had danced with her. "You have yet to sit out a dance, my lady, are you not tired?"

"Oh no, Your Grace. I was right, balls are most jolly. I feel I could dance forever."

Before he could reply, she crossed over to another gentleman, and a lady unknown to him stepped squarely on the instep of his foot

When the dance was over, he escorted Lady Maude back to her mother, thankful the pain in his foot had subsided. The next dance had been promised to his other sister, Esther. He was thankful that Esther had chosen the more sedate cotillion, for he doubted he was up to another quadrille.

After that he retired from the ballroom in favor of the anteroom, where several gentlemen were drinking their port, or brandy, and playing cards. He did not emerge until it was time to pick up his mother and sisters, and to thank the Garwoods for their gracious hospitality.

Six

Lucy had to wait to question Maude about the ball because she did not emerge from her bedchamber until well into the afternoon. Lucy could hardly stand the suspense. She had observed the festivities from the gallery that overlooked the ballroom, absolutely entranced by the opulence of the clothes and jewelry displayed below.

Maude finally joined her in the library. "I thought I would find you here. You always have your nose stuck in a book. If you are not careful, you will turn into one of those dreadful bluestockings and Miles will not want you."

Lucy felt her face grow hot. "What a peculiar thing to say. Miles and I are good friends, nothing more."

Maude laughed. "Surely you realize Miles has a *tendre* for you—at least he fondly imagines he has."

"I realize nothing of the sort, Maude, please stop teasing me. You are making me feel very uncomfortable."

"I am sorry, Lucy, I did not mean to. Please forgive me."

"Only if you tell me about the ball." Lucy was eager to put the exchange behind her.

"Where should I begin?" Maude put her forefinger to her cheek. "Let me see." She seemed to ponder for a moment, and then her eyes gleamed with mischief. "I suppose one could say the ball was a huge success. It was such a crush, the aged Lady Sinclair's wig was knocked awry. Terrible shade of red. She would have been far better off without it."

"Maude. I do not believe such gammon for a moment. Besides, you know very well it is not the story I wish to hear."

Maude grinned. "What aspect of the evening holds your interest The refreshments? The music? Surely not the music. I expect it could be heard clear across the square."

Lucy laughed in spite of herself. "I merely wished to know which of the young gentleman you danced with twice you liked the best. The one in the fine blue coat, or the Duke of Linborough all in black save for his silver brocade waistcoat? Who was the other one, by the way?"

"You were peeking?"

"Of course. The gallery offers a wonderful view of the entire ballroom. Incidentally, certain members of the *ton* behave in a very scandalous manner."

"*Now* who is telling stories?"

Lucy had second thoughts about robbing Maude of even a modicum of her innocence. "I was merely trying to repay you in kind for that dreadful business with the wig, and you have yet to tell me the name of Mr. Bluecoat."

"*Viscount* Bluecoat, if you please. Viscount Langley, to be precise. I found him to be much more amiable and handsome than the Duke of Linborough."

"That is not saying much. I rather think a bulldog would be more amiable than the gentleman in question. But perhaps not as handsome."

"That question is moot," Maude rejoined.

Both girls giggled uncontrollably at this piece of impertinence.

When the laughter finally died down, Lucy said, "Proceed with caution, Maude. Perhaps the viscount's charm was enhanced by the duke's lack thereof."

"I have every intention of doing so."

"Good." Lucy pondered the matter for a moment "Funnily enough, the Duke of Linborough had the right of it."

"Hmm?" Maude looked perplexed. "How do you mean?"

"Remember? At Gunter's? He said words to the effect that one's chances for happiness or misery were predicated on one's choice of a mate."

Maude shuddered. "Cheerful chap, is he not?"

"Most definitely not But joking aside, please be careful, Maude. Be very, very careful."

"Now that you mention it he did say something of the sort, but any good one might have derived from his advice was diminished by that dreadfully patronizing attitude of his."

"But are not all dukes top-lofty?"

"The ones who have all their faculties, I suppose. One or two of them are quite mad, you know. In any case, Lucy, do not let my brother foist anyone upon you for a husband you do not care for."

Lucy shrugged. "I daresay I shall never marry."

Maude's eyes widened. "But what will you do? Unless you are married you will know no true freedom. Spinsters are kept very fettered."

"Nonsense. I shall work at Hope House, and once I am old enough no one is going to bother about my comings and goings. I am sure I shall manage very well. Marriage will not be my only recourse."

As she uttered these words, a great weight lifted from her shoulders. Of course, that was it—James could certainly harbor no objections to her not marrying if she made herself useful at Hope House.

While Lucy and Maude discussed their futures, a conversation of a similar nature was taking place around the corner at the Duke of Linborough's own establishment. Robert and his mother had just finished a late breakfast and were leisurely sipping tea. Esther and Miriam had yet to stir from their beds, which suited him very well. Miriam was inclined to cackle when she laughed, and after a night of revelry, His Grace preferred to forego that doubtful pleasure.

"When you call on Lady Maude, I think you should take some flowers—nothing ostentatious, mind you—a little nosegay of violets would be nice."

Robert cast the duchess a jaundiced look. "For pity's sake, Mother, I have scarcely opened my eyes. Do you have to be so relentless in the pursuit of this matter?"

Martha Renquist's lower lip began to quiver. "I am sorry to

be such a trial to you, Robert. Heaven knows I forego many of life's little pleasures rather than burden you with any unreasonable demands." She punctuated this statement with a jagged sob and dabbed at her eyes with the corner of her handkerchief.

Rather than risk a floodgate of reproaches, Robert deemed it prudent to make amends. He leaned over the breakfast table and patted her hand. "I am sorry. I did not mean to imply such. It must have been dawn when we retired this morning, and quite frankly I am not up to this conversation as yet."

"Admit it, Robert, you will never be ready for this conversation because you have no intention of courting the Garwood girl."

"I will call on her—in a week or so. Give me time to catch my breath."

She glared at him, her lips compressed into a thin line. "By all means take your time. Is that not what you always do? I can see it now. You will go through the motions of courtship, but as usual, you will make sure that another claims her for a bride."

James felt his hackles rise. "I say. That is scarcely fair. I cannot help it if a girl prefers some other chap. What do you expect me to do? Drag one of them to the altar against her will?"

She fixed him with an icy stare, her eyebrows raised into inverted vees. "Do not play me for a fool, Robert. It will not work. Let me see. Last year there was Lady Margaret Alcroft—she married Lord Sinclair's heir, as I recall. Then the year before that, did you not dally long enough for Lady Frances Thistlethwaite to be snapped up? That would have been a brilliant match. As it is, the Garwood girl will do quite nicely."

"Will do quite nicely? I cannot believe my ears. Tell me, Mother, what happiness do you see for either party in such an arrangement? I heard no mention of love."

"No mention of love? Dear me, what has love got to do with marriage? Your bride has to be of impeccable lineage, worthy of your name, and capable of fulfilling the role of a duchess. Duty to family demands this of you."

"My father did not see it that way."

"What do you mean?"

"He married you because he loved you, did he not? I doubt he was concerned with your lineage at the time."

His mother turned pink. "How dare you say such a thing to me. I descend from baronies on both sides of my family. Why, one of my ancestors came over with William of Normandy."

Robert saw no reason to tell her that in medieval times the title of baron could be used by any town burger as a form of respect and did not necessarily carry a patent with it, and that all manner of petty knights followed the banner of William the Bastard during the conquest of England.

Her face hardened. "Let me put it to you this way, my son. Have you considered just what is out there in the marriage mart?"

"What do you mean?"

"The girls suitable for the position of Duchess of Linborough can be counted on one hand—that is, unless you wish to wait for some who are still learning their alphabets."

Robert's jaw dropped. "Surely you jest?"

"Of this year's crop, only two come to mind. The charming Lady Maude Garwood and the pimple-faced Lady Caroline Barclay. But perhaps you wish to wait until next year. I understand Lord and Lady Crestwood intend to thrust their daughter Ermentrude upon society."

Robert read the malice in her eyes. "Also pimple-faced, I daresay."

"Not at all." Her voice was deceptively sweet. Her smile even more so. "I am told Ermentrude has the complexion of a milkmaid."

"Well there you are." He breathed easier.

"Am I? Think. Think, Robert Lady Ermentrude Howard is the Earl of Crestwood's daughter, therefore—"

"Has no chin?" As he finished the sentence for her, he shuddered.

"Cheer up, Robert, it is not all that bad."

He should have known by her cheerful delivery that she was leading him into a trap, but too late he replied, "Chin not so bad, then?"

"I did not say that." Her voice dripped patience and

endurance. "I merely meant that what Lady Ermentrude lacks in chin, she makes up for in teeth."

"Teeth?"

She nodded. "Poor girl seems to have twice as many as anyone else."

Robert bowed to defeat "Say no more, Mother. Before the week is out, I shall present myself at Northwycke House, violets in hand."

Seven

With the specter of Lord Crestwood's daughter, Ermentrude, looming before him, Robert called at Northwycke House two days later, bearing a bouquet of daffodils and tulips for Lady Maude. A stubborn streak in his nature had eschewed his mother's suggestion of violets. After all, it would not do to have one's mother orchestrate one's courtship down to the last jot and tittle, now would it? One has to draw the line somewhere.

Robert expected to be taken into the intimate little reception room of his previous visit, but instead was ushered into the Garwoods' grand saloon, which to his dismay was already crowded with would-be suitors of Lady Maude's, interspersed with a sprinkling of older people.

An overpowering scent of roses assaulted Robert's senses. He perceived that every available surface in the room was banked with the precious hothouse blooms.

At first he was chagrined that his mother had suggested he bring an unpretentious posy. Even though he was not seriously pursuing the courtship of Lady Maude, he did not want to be seen in a bad light. Then he realized that one more bouquet of roses, among the many, was of no significance.

"How good of you to còme," said the younger Lady Northwycke, offering her hand.

"Not at all," he replied, kissing the air just above her gloved fingertips. "It is always a pleasure to be in such charming company."

The compliment was heartfelt. He could not for the life of him think how he had come to overlook the beauty of two Seasons ago. With her cameo-fair skin and luxuriant dark tresses, Emily Garwood possessed exactly the sort of beauty he admired in a woman. Then he recalled something of her background. Reared in genteel poverty, Miss Emily Walsingham would not have gained entrée into the circles in which he moved. He suffered a pang of regret.

Having been duly received by his charming hostess, he quickly scanned the room in search of Lady Maude. She was not difficult to find; her distinctive, low-pitched laugh could be heard rising amid a crush of attentive young swains. Suddenly, as if Moses had raised his staff, her sea of admirers parted, and Lady Maude came forward to acknowledge his arrival.

"Your Grace," she said, with the slightest of curtsies. "How do you do? It is so nice to see you."

Robert doubted it. Lady Maude was most probably a very poor card player, for beneath the polite pleasantry lurked a poorly concealed layer of ice. For some perverse reason, her attitude was a clarion call to the chase, and he became determined to have her melt in his arms before too long into the Season.

She buried her nose in his flowers. "Thank you, daffodils have such a heavenly scent. They are a most happy flower."

"Happy? How does one come to this conclusion?"

"How could one *not*, Your Grace? Yellow is the most joyous of colors, and when gracing the petals of a daffodil, can summer be far behind?"

Robert could not help but smile at her youthful enthusiasm. She was such a delightful creature. Lacking in depth, perhaps, but that was not necessarily a detriment. After all, she could have been one of those dreadful bluestockings. He dismissed the thought as too awful to contemplate.

With a slight bow he said, "Thank you for enlightening me. I shall never look at a daffodil in quite the same light again."

She smiled politely, but not before a look of skepticism flashed in her eyes. Robert bowed once more and moved to mingle with the crowd, leaving her to signal for a footman to relieve her of the flowers.

Robert worked his way through the guests, stopping to talk to this one and that, finally coming to a dead end at a large diamond-paned window. Having endured too many of such "at homes" while squiring his mother around London, he was thoroughly bored with the whole process.

Knowing the gardens at Northwycke were noted for their beauty, he glanced out the window. Unfortunately it overlooked the rose garden and the bushes, just beginning to leaf, were devoid of blooms. He saw what he took to be an undergardener on his hands and knees going about the task of pulling out newly sprouting weeds.

"Scrawny-looking chap," he muttered under his breath. "Does not look like there is much of him hiding under that smock he is wearing. Probably the only job he is good for."

Suddenly, the figure stood up to stretch and the sun glinted on a fiery halo of auburn hair. It was the Garwood girl. As if aware of being held under scrutiny, she turned and stared at him with her forthright brown eyes. Most of her face was smeared with mud, as if she had thoughtlessly rubbed her soiled hands across her face. The heavy wool smock she wore obscured the rest of her. This, too, bedaubed with mud.

This time Robert was the first to break eye contact with the girl. He turned his back to the window. He could not help but pity her. It seemed she was just as odd as the rest of the Shrewsbury Garwoods. Being a bluestocking was bad enough, but what normal young female would rather grub in the dirt like a pig seeking truffles, when she could be in an elegantly appointed saloon, partaking of pastries in the company of England's most eligible bachelors? After all, her cousin could only marry one of them and Robert had already decided he should be that one.

Maude's suitors were quickly narrowed down to Viscount Langley and the Duke of Linborough. Robert had made sure he was every bit as charming as the viscount.

He realized he had his work cut out for him during a carriage ride in Hyde Park with Lady Maude one fine sunny afternoon early in May. He had reined the horses to exchange pleasantries with a male acquaintance when he saw the strangest look cross his young companion's face. She was staring ahead with an expression that could only be described as stricken.

On following her gaze, he perceived Viscount Langley further down the path, astride a magnificent chestnut gelding. Beside him, a beautiful woman with flaxen hair peeking from beneath a stylishly plumed bonnet rode a dappled gray mare.

They took their leave of the passerby, and Lady Maude said, "If you please, I should like to go home now. I have this awful headache."

Deeming it politic to ignore the true cause of her discomfort, Robert offered his sympathy, then complied with her wishes. "I shall call on the morrow to see how you are faring," he said when making his departure, and right away he wished he had not made the offer. He did not relish the idea of trying to make conversation with a young lady pining away for someone else.

"How very kind of you, I am sure," she said in reply, the tone of her voice notably distracted.

He returned home considerably chastened. Was it possible the Garwood heiress actually preferred a suitor with a lesser title than himself? Incredible! The one time he deigns to venture into the marriage mart he hits a sticky wicket? It really was too funny for words, but he was not laughing. In truth, it was very hard to endure.

He was still in shock when he arrived home. The last thing he needed was the questioning look he received from his mother. If the determined glint in her eye was anything to go by, she was not about to let him off easily. He groaned inwardly.

When it came to his afternoon with Lady Maude, she would want to question him on every aspect. She would sift through every detail, lest some subtle nuance that would later prove to carry great significance escape her notice. In no mood to face the Grand Inquisitor, Robert decided on a direct approach.

"Do not get your hopes up, darling mater," he said. "I made a sincere effort to engage the affections of Lady Maude, and unlikely as it may sound, I rather believe the girl has lost her heart to Viscount Langley."

His mother's face registered a mixture of shock and disbelief. "She favors a callow youth over a man of consequence such as yourself?" Her tone was skeptical. "You are right, I find it most unlikely."

"But nevertheless, it is true." He went on to explain the incident in Hyde Park.

"But her reaction could merely be a manifestation of hurt pride," she said, seemingly loath to admit defeat.

"This is true. To take advantage of the situation, I failed to mention to her that the fair-haired beauty escorted by Viscount Langley happened to be his married sister, Agatha."

"How devious of you, and how clever."

"Why, Mother, I am shocked—one would think you were proud of what I did."

"Pish-posh. Unlike cricket marriage is not a sport. One does what one has to."

She began to pace the floor, hand to chin. Robert had not seen his mother so animated in a long time. She was actually enjoying herself! Suddenly she stopped pacing. "Tell me, Robert, is Lady Maude a very proper girl?"

"Good heavens, what a thing to ask. I would suppose so. She has never given me reason to think otherwise, and I have certainly conducted myself in a gentlemanly manner." He pondered this point for a moment. "Yes. I would have to say that Lady Maude is every inch the virtuous lady."

"And you have never kissed her?"

"Of course not," he said stiffly. "I resent the question."

She gave an impatient wave of her hand. "Pray do not be so tiresome, Robert. There is a purpose to all this."

"Be so good as to enlighten me."

"An innocent girl of great virtue is apt to fall in love with the very first man who has the audacity to kiss her."

Robert raised a brow. "Really? How came you by such knowledge?"

Her face colored. "Because it happened to me."

"So yours, and Father's, was a love match?"

He failed to notice that his mother did not answer him.

"So you are suggesting…?" he continued.

"You are not a fool, Robert, so kindly do not act like one. If you really want this sweet young thing for a wife, I suggest you kiss her to the point of suffocation—of course, there is always Lady Caroline Barclay..."

"Of the pimples?"

She nodded, the smile on her face a honeyed trap. "Look on the bright side, dear, pimples have been known to clear up after the birth of a second or third child."

Robert shuddered. "I doubt there would be a first—much less a third."

"Need I say more?"

Robert repaired to his bedchamber of the opinion that his mother had said more than enough, but try as he might he could not come up with a better strategy for winning the hand of the beauteous Lady Maude.

Lucy looked up from her needlework upon hearing Maude's footsteps crunch on the gravel path to the rose arbor. "Feeling better today?" Lucy posed the question without changing the rhythm of her motions as she plied a needle to the canvas stretched taut on the embroidery frame.

Maude looked mournful, "I doubt I shall ever feel better again. I had thought Viscount Langley to be sincere in his regard for me."

Lucy stayed her needle without completing the stitch. "Maude, do you not continue to see Lord Linborough?"

"I suppose. It keeps Mama happy."

"But if you bear no real affection for the gentleman, it is hardly fair to lead him on."

"I like him well enough. He is far more agreeable than we first thought." She paused to smile. "Unfortunately, unlike Viscount Langley, I have a feeling it takes considerable effort on his part." She paused again, as if searching her mind for something else to say. "He always plans such interesting amusements. Why, in a week or so, weather permitting, we are to go on a wonderful picnic at Richmond. There will be boating on the Thames and all manner of games."

"James would not permit you to do such a thing unless the rest of the family came along."

"And I would not entertain the idea of going without the family. We are all to attend, including you."

"I see. Then why are you so upset over seeing Viscount Langley with someone else?"

Maude began to pace. "I doubt you would understand. You see, I rather enjoy having them both dance attendance, each doing his best to please me."

"Are you sure then, that your reaction to seeing Viscount Langley with another lady is not unlike a small child not wanting to play with her dolly until another little girl takes a fancy to it?"

Maude stopped pacing and covered her mouth with her hand. "I had not thought so. You must think me a flighty creature."

"I think nothing of the sort," Lucy said stoutly. "I think you are the most good-hearted person I have ever known. It is only human to be upset by such an occurrence. The sense of betrayal must be devastating."

"Betrayed. Yes. That is exactly how I felt." Maude flung her arm across her forehead. "Betrayed," she repeated, adding considerably more drama to the utterance. "But even worse, it was as if someone I thought I knew and trusted suddenly became a stranger."

"Good heavens, Maude, you need to pull back on the racing ribbons a bit."

Maude stared at her. "What do you mean? Are we not speaking of betrayal?"

"I suggest you withhold judgment until you are sure of the facts."

"Hmmm?"

"Perhaps the lady was a friend or relation—most likely a guest of his parents whom he was obliged to squire to the park. After all, you were otherwise occupied."

Maude's face lit up. "Of course. Dear, sensible Lucy!" She gave her an impulsive hug.

"Ouch!" Lucy put a finger to her mouth.

"Oh dear. I made you prick yourself. I am so sorry."

"A mere trifle. I am quite used to being stuck with the wretched things. It did not even draw blood."

"Thank goodness. I should hate to think any got on your new dress. You look very lovely in it, the pale blue is most becoming and I just love the way the lavender sash is caught up under your bosom with the spray of violets. You have such a talent for putting the right colors together."

Lucy felt herself flush with pleasure. "It is so kind of you to say so. Your dress is also becoming. The little pink rosebuds look so well against the pale green."

Maude laughed. "Our coloring is so similar, whatever suits one should serve equally well for the other."

Maude smoothed the front of her dress and groaned. "Oh dear. My dress has a stain, I had not noticed. How provoking. His Grace will be here any moment now. Be a darling and keep him amused until I return."

"Keep him amused?" Lucy echoed. "My chances of walking on water would be far, far better."

"No matter," Maude said, blithely. "Do your best."

Lucy sighed, removed a book of poetry from a canvas bag and replaced it with her embroidery frame. "Very well, but take my needlework with you. The thought of having to entertain His Grace makes it impossible for me to sew another stitch."

75

Eight

The afternoon following his conversation with his mother, Robert decided to walk over to Mayfair Court. As he strode down the street he cut a very fine figure in his green frock coat and his pale beige pantaloons which showed off his long, well-muscled legs to good advantage. After listening to his mother's unorthodox views on courtship, he would lief have postponed the visit, however he had promised Lady Maude he would call to inquire after her health, and a gentleman always kept his word, did he not?

"I cannot for the life of me understand how the daughter of a clergyman could countenance such outrageous behavior, much less propose it," he muttered under his breath. "Although Lady Maude's lips *do* curve in a most enticing manner, almost begging to be kissed."

He stopped for a moment to contemplate the pleasure of kissing her, then threw up his hands. "What am I thinking? The whole idea is quite beyond the pale."

He continued to walk at a much faster pace and the imposing Northwycke house came into view, reminding him of the enormity of trifling with the sister of a man considered to be a nonpareil with both sword and pistol. In spite of his powerful build, Robert was more apt to be found in a library or attending the opera than settling a grudge on the grass at dawn.

"If I am to kiss his sister, it would be prudent to first ask for her hand." He became aware that he was talking out loud and with a furtive glance to make sure he had not been observed made his way through the gates of Northwycke House in tight-lipped silence.

"Lady Maude is in the garden, Your Grace," the butler

intoned. "I shall inform her of your presence."

"Never mind. I will join her."

The retainer bowed. "Very well, Your Grace, I believe you will find her in the rose garden. With the warm weather we have been enjoying of late, it is blooming quite nicely."

Robert nodded, forbearing to mention that the roses in his own garden were blooming in a similar state of nicety. Unlike the Garwoods, it had never been a tradition of the Renquists to indulge in chitchat with their servants.

He was drawn to an arbor of white roses by the sound of a lovely contralto voice singing a plaintive song of unrequited love. It was his experience that most young ladies would have been quick to display such an extraordinary talent, but he had never heard it mentioned that Lady Maude could sing.

He noticed her book lying neglected in her hand. Then she gave forth with a series of grace notes that made him gasp in admiration. When the song came to an end he plucked a rose from an overhanging bough and handed it to her.

With a diffident smile, she took it from him, then rose to her feet, her book falling to the ground as she did so. Robert was too entranced by her beauty to notice. Lady Maude had never looked lovelier. Her dress of pale blue muslin was most becoming. Furthermore, framed by tendrils of auburn curls, her face had a luminous quality he found most disturbing.

He approached her and raised her hands to his lips. They were perfumed with a floral scent he found most pleasant. "My lady," he murmured, "I am quite undone. Your beauty takes my breath away."

Her eyes widened into drowning pools and even as her lips parted in protest, his own claimed their sweetness. From the moment their lips touched, Robert felt a wholeness he had never experienced before, as if the emptiness in his heart and soul had finally been filled.

This feeling was followed by a passion of such force he could hardly stop his knees from buckling. He showered her face with tiny kisses, drinking of her essence with an ever-deepening thirst. But this did not suffice. He claimed her lips once more, at first nipping, then probing, and finally plundering, desperately reaching for the very core of her being.

At first she returned kiss for kiss, then with a sob she let go of the rose and pushed him away. Still caught up by the depth of his feelings he pulled her to him. "Please, Maude, I have never experienced such profound passion. I know you feel it too."

"For pity's sake, stop!"

This outburst was accompanied by a forceful shove, which almost knocked him over. He regained his balance just in time to espy the last scrap of blue muslin disappear around the corner of the rose arbor.

He stood frozen in openmouthed amazement. A female had never reacted to his kisses quite that way before, but then Lady Maude was the first innocent he had ever had the occasion to kiss.

"What was I thinking?" he uttered with a groan. The thought he might have ruined his chances with Maude was dismaying. "I must have been absolutely mad. Now I shall have to ask her brother's permission to pay my addresses posthaste and pray that in the meantime she does not apprise him of my disgraceful behavior."

As Lucy fled from the rose arbor her heart pounded so hard she thought it would burst. On entering the house, she sought refuge in the small room set aside for sewing. To her dismay, Miles Walsingham rose from a chair situated by the window.

From a remote place from within herself it seemed strange that she once harbored, if not a *tendre* for Miles, at least a romantic fantasy that one day he could be the answer to all of her problems.

But that was before she had shared kisses with Robot Renquist. Kisses which by the very joy and passion they had ignited in her served only to make her aware of her loss. All they could offer was a life of loneliness, devoid of bliss. They so falsely promised. Whereas the Duke of Linborough might wed a Lucinda Garwood, heiress of one of the Shrewsbury Garwoods, not for a moment would he countenance an alliance with Lucy Garwood, daughter of Gentleman Joe, the highwayman. Nor should he. The realization was bitter to swallow.

Miles's face lit up when he rose to greet her. "I say, Lucy, you look remarkably pretty in blue. You should wear it all the time. It does marvelous things for your complexion."

Lucy forced a smile. "Thank you, Miles. Although I should think one could grow awfully tired of wearing the same old color every day." She paused before continuing. "Er—I have noticed you have no difficulty telling Maude and me apart."

"Why should I? Maude is—er more—er whereas you are—"

"Less?"

"Kindly refrain from putting words in my mouth, young Lucy. I was going to say that you are more sylphlike."

The compliment warmed her. Miles was so agreeable, and so handsome. She clutched the faint hope that perhaps the Duke of Linborough had been toying with her when attributing great significance to his kisses. She gave Miles a speculative look.

Miles squirmed under her scrutiny. "What is it, Lucy? My cravat is not arranged correctly?" He nervously twiddled with the offending linen.

"Of course not. You are the very tulip of fashion."

He visibly glowed at the compliment. "What then?"

Lucy thought twice before plunging. "I was wondering if you would mind awfully doing me a fevor?"

"Just name it, dear girl. I would be most happy to oblige."

"Kiss me."

His eyes widened. "Did I hear you aright?"

"I rather expect so," she replied. "But if a kiss is too much to ask of you…"

"Good heavens, girl, I told you I would be delighted to do so—any chap in his right mind would be—but such a request is quite out of character. Perchance you will have the goodness to tell me what is behind all this?"

Lucy stood squarely before him, both hands on hips. "Stop your chattering and kiss me, Miles, or I shall find some other gentleman willing to do so." She turned to go.

Miles grabbed her arm. "Very well. I will do it—if only to keep you from the clutches of some bounder—but I think you have gone quite mad, you know."

He gave her a quick peck.

She stamped her foot. "Really, Miles, that simply will not do. Put some *effort* into it, if you please."

"I say, Lucy, I hope you know what you are doing. Personally, I do not feel at all right about this. It goes quite beyond the pale."

"Miles!" She placed a finger over his mouth. "If your kisses were as numerous as your words, this experiment would be over by now."

"Experiment? Is *that* what this is? An experiment?"

Lucy nodded.

"Forgive me. That makes all the difference."

"There is no need for sarcasm. Either kiss me, or go home."

"If those are my choices, Lucy Garwood, you have only yourself to blame."

He reached out for her, a determined glint in his eye. This was a side of Miles she had never seen before and she felt no longer in control. Before she could offer a protest, his lips were on hers, probing, claiming.

Lucy broke away. "Thank you, Miles. I am obliged to you."

"Experiment over?" He looked like a crestfallen puppy.

She nodded. "I am sorry, Miles. It was wrong of me to ask it of you."

She patted his cheek and was about to leave the room when he caught her hand and bestowed a kiss upon it. "Do not be sorry, Lucy. Kissing you was most pleasant."

"And nothing more?"

"Should it be?" Miles sounded genuinely puzzled.

Lucy sighed. "Probably not."

"In which case, I had better be going before you come up with another harebrained scheme to make me look foolish. I had hoped to find James at home."

"Oh?"

"Yes. I wanted his advice on an investment that I was considering. Perhaps I shall catch up with him later at White's. He usually plays cards with some of his Peninsula cronies on Tuesdays."

Miles took his leave with the courtliest of bows, leaving Lucy to wish the Duke of Linborough had never kissed her; indeed, she rued ever having met him. His Grace had told the truth. What they had shared went beyond kisses, which meant that his loss must have been as great as her own.

She was about to depart for her bedchamber when Maude, looking as fresh as a daffodil in a dress of yellow lawn, entered the room brandishing Lucy's book.

"I say. What happened? I returned to the garden to find this lying in the dirt and positively no sign of you or His Grace. Has he not arrived? It is not like him to keep a lady waiting."

Lucy concealed crossed fingers within the folds of her dress. "He stayed just long enough to inquire after your health." She told herself it was not a complete lie. His Grace *did* stay long enough to express an interest in Maude's health. It served no purpose for her to know he had not actually *done* so.

Once within the confines of her own chamber, Lucy leaned with her back to the door, tears streaming down her face. "If only you had not kissed me," she whispered between sobs. "I would have been quite content with those I shared with Miles. After all, as he said, they were quite pleasant. Now, I suppose I shall spend my days working with the children at Hope House with no hope of ever having any of my own."

Nine

On returning home, Robert retired to his chambers and did not put in an appearance for the evening meal, preferring to dine in solitude. He had no desire to subject himself to a barrage of questions and recriminations by his mother on his ineptitude in kissing young girls to the point of suffocation. Indeed, from the amount of lung power Lady Maude had applied protesting his efforts, he would hazard the task was quite beyond his capabilities.

This knowledge weighed heavily on his mind. Be it in a rose arbor, a goosedown bed, or on top of a mountain, for that matter, Robert knew that for him a lifetime of kissing those enticing lips would not be enough.

After a restless night, he rose at first light. His valet showed a great lack of enthusiasm for helping him dress. In fact, with eyes heavy from insufficient sleep, he swayed in front of Robert, a razor in his hand.

Robert waved him away. "For heaven's sake, Sanders, return to your bed before you cut my throat. I will do until after breakfast."

A look of extreme relief reflected on the manservant's face. "My apologies, Your Grace, but I think it would be for the best." He lost no time in bowing himself out of Robert's dressing room.

To Robert's annoyance, his early arrival in the morning room was cause for considerable consternation among his staff.

"Breakfast will take a while, Your Grace. I am afraid we were not expecting you to rise so early," the butler said, a flustered look on his face.

"Do not fuss, Palmer. A cup of tea and some of that

chicken from last night's dinner will suffice—that is, if there is any left. It was absolutely delicious."

"As you wish, Your Grace."

Nevertheless, in spite of Robert's willingness to partake of a makeshift breakfast the meal was not forthcoming with any great haste, and when it did arrive, it proved to be a sumptuous affair carried into his presence in huge, silver dishes with full pomp and ceremony by a cavalcade of footmen. In other words, a proper English breakfast fit to put before a duke of the realm.

Robert gave Palmer a questioning look.

The butler avoided eye contact, choosing to aim his focus somewhat to the left of Robert. "Ahem! Unfortunately, sir, Cook could not be persuaded to serve the chicken."

Robert shrugged and sat in the chair the man held out for him. Ever since the Prince Regent had personally complimented Cook on the salmon in aspic she had prepared for his last visit, her culinary skills had grown in leaps and bounds. Unfortunately, so had her sense of self-worth. The woman had become as temperamental as an opera singer.

As he relished a dish of pork chops and kidneys, savoring the subtle seasonings she had added to the sauce, he had to admit that the meal had been well worth the waiting. He ate every delicious morsel, drained his cup, and was in the process of patting his mouth with a napkin when his mother bustled into the room.

He smothered a groan. He had hoped to get out of the house long before she came downstairs. He started to rise, but she waved him down. One of the footmen helped seat her at the table.

She beckoned to Palmer. "Please see to it that my breakfast is served, then kindly clear the room. I wish to speak to His Grace in private."

Once they had the room to themselves, the duchess took a few mouthfuls of food, then put down her fork. Robert steeled himself for what was about to follow; his mother did not forego the pleasures of the table for idle chitchat unless entertaining guests. He attributed this foible to the frugal meals she had suffered growing up as the daughter of a lowly curate.

"I am assuming that yesterday did not go as well as we had hoped?"

"Why would you assume anything of the sort, Mother?" Robert parried, delaying the inevitable recriminations as long as possible.

She beamed. "Then everything went well?"

"I did not say that."

She pouted. A network of lines furrowed her upper lip, taking away any pretension she might have had of clinging to her youth. "Do not be difficult, dear. It is not good of you." She let out a sigh. "Heaven knows I do not deserve such ill usage."

Not wishing to endure a threnody of the injustices she was preparing to accuse him of, he hastened to assure her of his full cooperation. "Do not upset yourself, Mother. I kissed Lady Maude. I had not intended to, but the thought was put into my head, and there you are—it happened. Or perhaps because she looked uncommonly pretty yesterday morning I could not help myself. In any case, I am inclined to think that in the doing, I made a complete cake of myself."

"Robert! Surely you are mistaken?"

He shrugged. "Afraid not. At first I thought she was receptive to my advances, but such was not the case."

"One cannot be sure. Perhaps she was showing maidenly reticence—that is not entirely a bad thing—in fact to the contrary, it shows she will prove to be a virtuous wife."

"If maidenly reticence includes yelling, 'For pity's sake, stop,' at the top of her lungs and almost knocking me down in an effort to get away, I suppose one could say that."

She looked crestfallen. "Oh, dear me. I see what you mean." Then her face brightened. "You must not take this setback to be a personal rejection."

"No? How do you see it, pray tell?"

"Sarcasm does not become you, Robert. She is a young female of delicate sensibilities, and your advances frightened her. Pray do not kiss her again, at least not until she agrees to marry you." His mother gestured, her fingers outstretched like a coquette's fan. "It would be prudent to act as if it had never happened. Be more circumspect."

"Just how am I supposed to go about it? Before I made a fool of myself, I liked to think I was the very soul of circumspection, and much good did it do me."

"Hush for a moment, and let me think." Her brow knitted. "In the first place, we have to get Viscount Langley from underfoot." She snapped her fingers. "But of course! We shall invite the Garwoods to stay with us at Linborough Castle. That way you shall be constantly thrown together."

"That will make her receptive to my suit?"

She pinched his cheek. "Of course it will, darling. Given time, she cannot help but develop a *tendre* for you."

Robert leaned over and kissed her forehead. "I hope you are right, but I fear mother love robs you of all discernment. Nevertheless, I shall issue the invitation to the Garwoods forthwith. You see, Mother, I have come to the conclusion that Lady Maude suits me very well."

Maude folded her arms in front of her. Lucy knew this boded no good and wished she had not had the misfortune to be in her company when James entered the library to inform his sister of the invitation to Linborough Castle.

"I am supposed to endure the Duchess of Linborough's company for a fortnight? James, how could you?"

"It is Mother and I who will have to endure her nonsense— Emily wishes to stay home with our son. I suppose I shall enjoy some occasional angling with His Grace, it is too early for a pheasant shoot, but for the main, he will be entertaining you— Lucy will accompany you, of course."

Lucy gave a start. "Surely not? I rather thought I should return to Northwycke Hall to help with the babies at Hope House. The nursemaids scarcely have time for their most basic of needs."

"Nonsense. If such is the case, I shall see to it that another nursemaid is hired before we leave for Linborough. Maude cannot go haring all over the countryside without a chaperon."

Lucy was tempted to point out that Smith, Maude's abigail, had always served as chaperon, but felt it would show a dreadful lack of gratitude on her part not to cooperate. She bowed to the inevitable. "In that case, I shall be only too pleased to oblige."

"Well I am not." Maude looked as truculent as a two-year-old. "I am not entirely sure that I am receptive to the Duke of Linborough's suit. I find Viscount Langley to be much more amusing."

"That is all very well, Maude, but I have observed a certain lack of perseverance in the viscount's courtship. On the other hand, His Grace is much more attentive and thoughtful in his efforts to please you."

"That is the problem, James. You have made it patently clear that you favor the duke's suit over his own. I truly believe, that Viscount Langley has lost all hope of gaining your approval."

"If the young man is not willing to put his heart and soul into winning your hand, Maude dear, one has to conclude he is unworthy of the prize."

"Do not be so horrid, James. You twist everything I say to use against me."

He patted her shoulder. "I do not mean to. I think you might be making a mistake, but if it is your wish, Maude, I shall decline the invitation. Heaven knows I was not looking forward to the excursion."

Before Maude could reply, there was a discreet knock on the door and the butler entered, bearing a silver salver.

"If you please, sir, Viscount Langley called while Lady Maude was out and left this letter for her."

Maude took it from him. "Thank you, Hobbes." She waited for the servant to leave before breaking the seal. She hesitated before opening it and addressed James. "Would you mind awfully if I read it?"

"By all means, go right ahead."

Maude read the letter twice before looking up. "Under the circumstances, I think we should accept the Linboroughs' kind invitation." Her voice was tight and full of hurt. "It appears that

Viscount Langley delivered this before departing for Scotland. Evidently someone is stirring up trouble with the workers on an estate his family owns up there."

James reached out to her. "I am sure he would not have gone if it were at all avoidable."

She smiled at him. Lucy saw the tears glistening in her eyes. "I am afraid I cannot agree. As you implied, the gentleman is unworthy of the prize." Her chin raised. "At no time did he bother to mention his family had any ties to Scotland—I wonder what else he deemed not worth the telling? In fact, I doubt I knew Viscount Langley at all." With a muffled sob, she fled the room.

Lucy motioned to follow her, but James put a restraining hand on her shoulder.

"Let her go. She will not thank you for seeing her that way. Some tears are not for sharing—at least not right away."

Lucy excused herself and repaired to her own chamber, distressed by her cousin's unhappiness. She had watched the pleasure slowly drain from Maude's face as she read the viscount's letter, and would have willingly accepted the burden of it in her stead.

Lucy flung herself on the bed. "Poor, poor Maude," she murmured into the pillow. "She has never known a day's unhappiness in her life and is ill-equipped to deal with it."

Save your sorrow for yourself. Maude will most likely marry the only man you could possibly love. The little voice in her head mocked her, totally devoid of sympathy.

Lucy pounded the pillow with her fists, then threw it across the room. Feeling remorse, she left the bed to retrieve it, then hugging it to her chest went to the window and looked outside, tears glistening on her cheeks.

The window overlooked the street. Through a blur of tears she observed a young girl walking in the shade of the plane trees that overhung the fence of the private park the Garwoods shared with the other residents of Mayfair Court. She wore a dress of brown homespun, and a large basket of fruit burdened her bony frame.

Upon reaching the gates of Northwycke House, she stopped and began to sing. Her voice rang true and clear, a quality to be found in only the very young.

"Cherries ripe. Cherries ripe. Please buy nay cherries. Be ye full or be ye fair, please buy my ripe cherries."

Lucy felt for the waif. If Mickey Dempsey had not come to her aid, she would have been in a similar situation, or worse. She could very well have suffered the same fate as her mother and be lying in a pauper's grave.

"If dear James did nothing else for me," she whispered, "I shall be eternally grateful that he reunited Mama and Papa at Saint Anne's."

Castigating herself for the shameful indulgence of self-pity she was displaying, she watched the girl shiver as a sudden breeze whipped at her skirts, affording Lucy a glimpse of ragged petticoat. Lucy turned away. To her dismay, no amount of pity for the other girl seemed to lessen her own grief.

Ten

Linborough Castle rose from the cliffs along the Dorset coast, proud and indomitable. Since the very first stones were raised, to its present day grandeur of towers and turrets, it had never fallen to an enemy.

Maude stuck her head out of the carriage window to get a better view. "I say, it is every bit as beautiful as Arundel Castle, and, I would venture a trifle larger." She turned her head. "Would you not agree, Mama?"

"Certainly not. There can be no comparison. This castle has not had a curtain wall for centuries. Close that window immediately and try to comport yourself as befits a lady of your station. I shudder to think that the Linboroughs might have seen you."

"Oh, Mama, do not take away my fun. It is bad enough we have to come here in the first place."

"I suggest that before you leave this carriage you dispense with your disgraceful attitude. I will not have you bringing shame upon your brother's good name."

Maude slumped back into her seat. "It is all very well for James. For the most part, it has been sunny and he has been able to ride. We, on the other hand, have been jostled in this stuffy coffin for the better part of three days."

"Do not be such an ingrate, Maude. James made this journey for your sake. I am sure he would far rather be at Northwycke with Emily and James Elias."

"So would I, Mama, so would I."

"Do try to show a little sense. Any other young lady would love to be in your shoes."

"Any other young lady may *have* my shoes any time she

wishes. I find this all so humiliating. I know this has been planned so the Duke of Linborough can make up his mind as to whether or not he wants me for his duchess. It just will not do, Mama. I value myself far higher than that."

Her mother fixed Maude with an icy stare. Lucy cringed at the thought of what was to follow, but Maude seemed too angry to care.

"Oh? Just how high do you aspire, young lady?" Lady Northwycke's voice dripped acid. "Royalty marries royalty, not impertinent young snips who overstep themselves."

Maude scowled. "You deliberately misunderstand me, Mother. I care not for a man's rank, I just despise being looked over like so much horseflesh."

The dowager bit her lip. "I should not be telling you this, but the truth cannot make your attitude any worse than it is."

Maude sat up straight. "Tell me what, Mama?"

"His Grace has made it known to James that he wishes your hand in marriage."

"Then what is the reason for this tiresome trip?"

"Are you saying you would accept his offer?"

Maude sighed. "Why does everyone want to spoil everything by marrying me off in my very first Season?"

"You did not answer my question."

Maude folded her arms across her chest, her mouth set in a stubborn line.

"I see. The Duke of Linborough is hoping that given time, you will find his company pleasant enough to make his castle your home. But I think he would do better to look elsewhere. Your behavior does little to recommend you to any man, much less a duke."

"I am sorry, Mama. I know you mean well. I am not a complete fool, but I will not—no—cannot marry a man I do not love."

"Is there someone else? Viscount Langley, perhaps?"

"Certainly not," Maude snapped. "He is an inconsiderate boor, severely lacking in the qualities I require in a husband."

"Then it is possible that His Grace could win your heart?"

"I daresay."

Lucy could scarcely credit Maude's offhand response. How could she *not* love the man? Lucy dug her fingernails into the palms of her hands in a vain effort to deaden her grief. Would that he were a country squire, or even a lowly footman, if it would mean she could devote the rest of her life to loving him.

Suddenly Maude leaned forward, all ill humor wiped from her countenance like chalk from a slate. Lucy knew then. Maude had decided to reject the duke, but in the interim was not going to let it prevent her from enjoying his hospitality. She fought the urge to give the lighthearted Maude a good shaking.

"Oh I say." Maude was now imbued with an air of gaiety. "His Grace is riding out to meet us on the most beautiful white horse I have ever seen. He should be clad in armor of burnished gold, mounted on such a steed."

Lucy wondered if seeing His Grace in such a heroic light would not make Maude fall in love after all. The thought made her stomach lurch. She was tempted to look out the window to get a glimpse of her beloved, but refrained. To make matters worse, Maude's mother was eyeing her suspiciously.

"Is anything the matter, child? You look as if you have seen a ghost."

"I thank you for your concern, madam, but no, there is nothing the matter."

"Hmmph. You do not look well."

It was as much as Lucy could do to refrain from squirming under her scrutiny.

"The way you have taken to dressing your hair of late does not help matters. Whatever possesses you to pull it back in that tight little bun? Really, Lucy, it is hard for a sixteen-year-old girl to look like an old maid, but you seem to have managed it rather well."

"Mama is right. You do not even look like yourself. I do not mean to be unkind, Lucy darling, but that horrid bun takes away all your prettiness."

"It serves my purpose. It is easy to do and no one at Linborough Castle will care." Even as she spoke, Lucy felt a heaviness crushing her spirit. Indeed, why should anyone care a fig how she looked?

This topic came to an end when James and the duke steadied their mounts, one on each side of the carriage. Lucy held her breath, terrified he would realize it was she whom he had kissed in the rose arbor. On a deeper level she yearned for him to recognize her and make a declaration of his eternal love. The brief nod he tossed her before making Maude the focus of his attention dashed water on this vain dream.

Awash in misery, Lucy watched him pay court to Maude. It seemed he wanted her opinion on diverse subjects and reacted to her lighthearted responses with what Lucy perceived to be a resigned little smile.

In spite of her own feelings toward their host, Lucy wished Maude could have attached more depth to her answers, then she dismissed the thought. Did not gentlemen prefer their wives to be mere ornaments, casting no shadows on their own glory? Lucy breathed easier for her kinswoman. His Grace was a prime example of the prideful aristocrat not likely to brook any challenge to his place in the scheme of things. Maude would most likely make him an admirable wife—if she so chose.

As the carriage lumbered up the winding road to the castle grounds, followed by two lesser conveyances carrying their luggage and body servants, Lucy kept her gaze on the ancient yews bordering their way. Her eyes widened when their host informed them they had been planted almost four hundred years previously to spruce up the place in anticipation of a visit from mad King Henry the Sixth, in one of his more lucid periods.

"Of course," the duke added, "the place underwent considerable transformation about a century ago, thanks to the genius of Sir John Vanbrugh. Now you ladies can be transported by carriage all the way to the front door. In the old days, you would have had to finish the last leg of your journey by litter."

"Thank goodness for small mercies," Lady Northwycke muttered under her breath. Out loud, she said, "Some people think, and I am inclined to agree, that Linborough is indeed the flower of Sir John Vanbrugh's career, superseding even his masterpiece, Castle Howard, in magnificence."

The duke beamed. "Why, thank you, my lady. How very kind of you to say so. I like to think I have made a few improvements of my own."

"So I have heard," James interjected. "I assume you are referring to the baths and—er—other conveniences you had installed in some of the anterooms of the larger suites? I understand they are marvels of engineering."

The duke nodded.

"I have been thinking of making some improvements at Northwycke."

Lucy was in awe. She had grown up in rented rooms, where baths were taken in a battered old tub in the washhouse, and the necessary was an odiferous little shed at the bottom of a narrow back garden. She thought the facilities at Northwycke to be most impressive, and could not imagine how they could be improved upon.

The shock she received upon being ushered into the large reception hall of the castle was absolutely staggering. Northwycke Hall was considered to be one of the finest houses in England, but it did not prepare her for the opulence of the country seat of the Renquists.

Her first impression was a dazzle of gold rococo on every surface, including the elaborate balustrades flanking the huge staircase dominating the room. It seemed to her that a parade of soldiers could traverse its flight with plenty of room to spare. This was crowned by a huge, domed ceiling on which was painted a scene depicting St. George slaying a fire-breathing dragon, while a host of encouraging angels hovered over him.

Privately, Lucy thought the beautiful maidens and the plump cherubs adorning the ceiling at Northwycke Hall were more pleasing, but nevertheless this was a spectacle she had never expected to see. Not in her wildest dreams had she imagined being a guest of someone as top-lofty as the Duke of Linborough. Under normal circumstances, it was doubtful she would even gain entrée to the servants' quarters.

She spent the rest of the day in a daze. She lagged behind

the others while they were being led through a long enfilade of sun-drenched staterooms in order to take in her fill of myriad treasures, from the gallery of family portraits painted by the masters of each generation, to highly polished furniture, some inlaid with brass and mother-of-pearl.

Every surface displayed treasures of infinite beauty and every corner boasted statues of bronze and marble perched on fluted columns of polished mahogany, or deeply veined marble.

She stood absolutely entranced before a Dresden figurine of a little shepherdess. She remembered reading that the last Queen of France, the lighthearted Marie Antoinette, used to enjoy idylls in the countryside arrayed in such costumes—and paid dearly for the privilege. Lucy suddenly felt cold. Even a queen cannot be assured of a safe and happy life—why should she expect more?

Suddenly startled by the sensation of a hand on her shoulder, she turned to find herself locked in the gaze of her host's blue eyes.

"I see that you admire the little shepherdess. It is one of my favorite pieces."

"Indeed, I do, Your Grace, although it also makes me feel a trifle sad."

He raised a brow. "Oh? How so?"

"I cannot help but think of poor Queen Marie Antoinette. How after a life of pursuing make-believe dreams, she suffered such a nightmarish end."

"How odd. I myself have thought the very same thing while contemplating the piece, but until now have never heard anyone else express such an opinion." He patted her cheek. "At your age your imagination should dwell on more pleasant subjects. Try not to think so hard, young Lucy."

Her heart sang. When he had referred to her as "young Lucy," rather than Miss Garwood had she detected a certain warmth in his tone? Her inner voice warned her against the folly of such fancies. Even if His Grace were to fall on his knees and declare eternal devotion, it would be to no avail.

Her musings were cut short by the arrival of Maude. "Oh,

there you are, Lucy. What kept you?"

"I was admiring the little shepherdess."

Maude bent over to inspect it. "Ah yes. Such a pretty little thing. I just love the white lace on the sleeves and those darling little rosebuds at the waist."

His Grace smiled at Lucy over Maude's bent figure. "You see? Lady Maude has the proper attitude. I doubt she stays awake at night bothered by dark thoughts."

Lucy felt as if she had been stripped bare. How could he possibly know of her sleepless nights, and the fears that made them so? Then it occurred to her it was because he also possessed a nature that afforded him little rest.

Lucy and Maude were given adjoining chambers, vast rooms with coffered ceilings and wall coverings of Chinese silk brocade, depicting exotic pastoral scenes of the Far East. Warmed by the glow of their friendship, they stood in front of the huge, floor-to-ceiling window in Lucy's room and viewed the ocean glistening in the early evening sun.

Lucy gazed in awe. "I had no idea the sea was so beautiful."

"Really? I thought you grew up near the water."

"Oh, no. Only until I reached nine. That is why life for us was such a struggle. We would have had plenty to sustain us with the rag-and-bone trade had we not moved away from the docks, which, incidentally, are on the Thames, not the ocean. Papa insisted on renting rooms in Bloomsbury. Not the best part of that district, mind you, but adequate.

"Of course, Mama and I could not stay there after Papa died. We went back to the old district, but Mickey feared for our safety and insisted we leave." She gave a bitter laugh. "Besides, we could not afford to stay there. The most miserable hovel Limehouse had to offer was beyond our means. That is why we ended up working in that horrid little garret."

Maude gave her hand a sympathetic squeeze. "You will never be in such a position again. Even Bloomsbury does not sound very nice."

"In a way, our stay there turned out to be fortunate for me. A gentleman scholar had the rooms below ours, and he taught me Latin and Greek and a smattering of philosophy. I would not trade that experience for anything."

Maude looked mystified. "Why would you want to study such dreary subjects?"

"Because I could."

Maude shook her head. "We may look alike, but rest assured, Lucy, had the choice been mine, I doubt I should have learned anything, save music and dancing."

Lucy laughed. "Dr. Fielding was scarcely proficient in such subjects. But you like to read."

"Yes. Reading can be pleasant, providing one stays away from ponderous subjects."

"And one day you might want to pour out your passion on paper to some lucky gentleman."

Maude broke out in giggles. "Do you really think so? Sometimes I wonder if I have the depth to feel passion—much less put it to paper."

Lucy took her hand. "Maude, girls like you thrive on love. Do not settle for anything less."

Maude put her other hand over Lucy's. "I think, dear niece, in that, we are very much alike. It is my heartfelt wish that you find a gentleman worthy of your love."

They watched the sky turn to fire, washing the distant Isle of Wight in a rosy glow. Being summer, it was still light when, at eight o'clock, it was time to join the others for dinner.

Robert spent the next few days taking Maude and Lucy on walks along the cliffs. His own sisters accompanied them the first time or two, then begged off, claiming the endeavor had left them with blisters on their heels.

He noticed Lucy took care to keep her distance, barely serving in her position as chaperon. She would stop to pick wildflowers, or peer over the edge of the cliffs ostensibly to inspect the seagull nests ensconced in the nooks and crannies of the rocks.

When he grew bored with Maude's innocent chatter, he

would retrace his steps to hurry Lucy along. After he had done this several days in a row, he stopped short. *Horror of horrors. Could it be that I actually prefer the company of this dowdy bluestocking over that of the beauteous Lady Maude?* he wondered.

Not for everything. Good heavens. Why would I want to invite such a strange creature to my bed? Or yet engage the delectable Maude in intellectual discourse? The latter's talents promise to be more voluptuary in nature. Those kisses. Would they transport me so, if I did not love her? No. Once I convince the adorable girl to become my bride, our happiness is assured.

With this thought in mind, he joined Lucy at the edge of the cliff. "Ah. Here you are," he said. Even as he uttered the words, he acknowledged their redundancy. He peered over the edge and wondered what held her interest, for he saw nothing out of the ordinary.

"I was very intrigued by your opinions regarding the philosopher Epicurus," he continued. "Your tutor must have been a student of Dr. Fielding's, one of the most brilliant men ever to grace the hallowed halls of Oxford."

Lucy stooped to pick a stalk of grass. Robert had the impression she did this to buy time before responding to his statement. Such a strange girl. What possible difference could it make who had tutored her—or why, for that matter? Although it would be an unlikely subject for most females, he had to own that Lucy Garwood was not like any other girl he had ever met. Large dowry notwithstanding, few men would be willing to take on such an oddity.

She straightened up and cast the grass stalk to the ground. There was a trace of defiance in the gesture, which carried over into her voice. "Dr. Fielding *was* my tutor."

"Really? I do not question your veracity, child, but the man resigned his post at Oxford right about the time I came down, and has not been heard from since."

"He made mention of that. Said he grew tired of wasting his time tutoring the offspring of the Philistines—it took too much time away from his work."

"Which is?"

"Writing a comprehensive study on every philosopher known to man. The last time I saw him, which was in the autumn, two years ago, he was up to Montaigne, and having a thoroughly good time in the doing."

"Er—yes, I should imagine. Montaigne could be a trifle earthy." Privately, Robert was somewhat aggrieved. He had fondly imagined he had achieved some degree of rapport with his erstwhile professor, indeed, he had even made a futile effort to trace his whereabouts when he had dropped from sight.

"But I digress. Am I to understand that while spurning to teach some of the future leaders of this country, he deemed a young girl worthy of his tutorial? I mean no offense, but it does not make sense."

Lucy grimaced. "The professor owned as much, in fact, he deemed my being born a female an utter waste. He rather fancied I could have followed in his footsteps if it had been otherwise. Personally, I am inclined to think he allowed his personal regard for my family to color his opinion."

Robert shook his head. "If Dr. Fielding considered you to be worthy of his time and attention, rest assured, he knew whereof he spoke."

Personally, he thought the scholar had done the young girl a great disservice by singling her out for special attention. After having glimpsed such a Pandora's box of knowledge, how could she possibly be satisfied with the restrictions society imposed upon her by reason of her gender? Robert concluded she faced a difficult life ahead, for the traditional role of a woman would not fit her too well.

The Garwoods' visit to Linborough was in its second week, and Robert had yet to propose to Maude. In spite of the kisses he had shared with her under the rose arbor, he could detect no answering warmth in her attitude and she was too well chaperoned for him to try to rekindle the fires. He regretted having invited some of the neighbors over for the evening, for he deemed they would take away any intimacy he could have hoped for.

He encountered his two sisters on the way down the stairs

and was taken by what he perceived to be a great improvement in their appearances.

Esther had taken on an air of classic elegance. Her hair was sleekly styled, the only ringlets cascading down the back, away from her face, and she was simply gowned with not a frill or a flounce in sight. Miriam, on the other hand, had two lovelocks swirling forward to disguise her heavy jaw, and her dress was also of an elegant simplicity, the trimmings smaller in scale than she usually sported.

He complimented them. "You both look exceedingly pretty this evening."

They glowed.

"Do you really think so?" Miriam asked.

"Oh, quite. You both look so well put together."

Esther sighed. "I am rather inclined to think that Mama was not too pleased. She is most put out with what she termed, 'Miss Garwood's unseemly interference.'"

"Miss Garwood advised you as to your attire?"

Ruth giggled. "I know what you are thinking. How could that mouse possibly advise *anyone* on such subjects as beauty and dress?"

Robert grinned. "I would not have couched it quite so bluntly, sister dear—but yes, such a thought comes to mind"

"After Lady Maude assured us that she found her cousin's advice invaluable in such matters, we thought it would not hurt to at least listen to what she had to say."

"Which was?"

"In my case," said Esther, "she suggested I get rid of all the little-girl flounces. She said, 'If you are tall, *be* tall.'"

"Hmm." Robert murmured "One has to admit, Esther, that she has transformed you into something quite magnificent."

"And she told *me*, 'If you are small, be small.' She altered our dresses with her own hands. Madame Duprés's establishment does not turn out finer work. The girl is an absolute treasure."

Robert was bemused. "Next, you will be telling me that she has also taken to dressing your hair."

"Of course not," Esther snapped. "The very idea. But she

did advise our abigails how to go about it."

"It is unfortunate that Miss Garwood is of the *ton;* she would make an absolute treasure of an abigail," Miriam interjected with a gleeful little titter.

Robert raised a brow. "Why, you little ingrate, you sound positively malicious." He softened this remark by bending low to bestow a kiss upon her cheek. Kissing the statuesque Esther took a lot less effort. Both sisters showed their pleasure by each taking one of his arms and allowing him to escort them down the stairs.

Dinner proved to be a long, drawn-out affair with too many courses and too much wine, and when the gentlemen finally joined the ladies in the drawing room, a very indifferent game of crambo was winding down. His mother shot Robert a look of relief.

She raised a hand to her throat, an act which displayed her jeweled fingers to advantage, and with much fluttering of her eyelids said, "Perhaps you gentlemen will rescue us. La. I am afraid our poor attempts at rhyming have descended to the depths of inanity."

"Come now, Your Grace, I am sure you exaggerate. In this room is assembled the best of womanly beauty England has to offer. Each a living poem in her own right"

The deliverer of this flowery prose was the Earl of Kincannon, a Scottish lord who was visiting his son, Viscount Rossmere, Robert's closest neighbor. The earl was a florid man in his sixties, who, although his portly shape strained his pantaloons to the limit, showed every sign of considering himself to be God's gift to the feirer sex.

"Oh, for heaven's sake, you old fool, hold your weesht to cool your porridge," his countess muttered under her breath.

It seemed that everyone heard her except her husband, for whereas the rest of them exchanged glances of both shock and amusement, the earl appeared to be totally oblivious. Robert concluded that mercifully the old gentleman was deaf, and too vain to use a horn.

Robert decided to deflect attention away from the

Kincannons. "Perhaps Lady Maude will grace us with a song."

To his surprise, Lady Maude's face flushed a rosy red. "Oh, no, I beseech you!" she exclaimed, "I have a very indifferent singing voice."

He attributed the blush to her remembrance of their encounter in the garden at Mayfair. *Such a modest maiden in spite of her frivolous ways*, he thought. This was a good trait in a prospective wife.

When she was finally persuaded to sing, he had to admit she was telling the truth. She had a pleasant contralto singing voice, but nothing singular. Any number of young girls within their circle of friends could acquit themselves equally as well. He concluded she lacked the self-confidence to sing in public.

After Maude's performance drew to a close and her audience had politely applauded, her mother addressed the countess. "I trust your journey from Scotland was pleasant?"

The lady rolled her eyes to the ceiling. "Such a journey is always arduous. This will be our last. In future, if our son wishes to see us, he shall have to come to Kincannon."

"Anything interesting to report among our Scottish friends?" Lady Northwycke continued.

"Not too much. I believe Viscount Langley was expected to pay a visit to our neighbors, the Douglases. It is speculated that he was coming to ask for their daughter Flora's hand."

Lady Northwycke's brows arched. "Really?"

"Oh, yes."

It was evident to Robert that the countess was elated at being able to impart such news.

"It is common knowledge in our parish that an alliance between the young ones has been the fond wish of both families ever since the pair were in leading strings. Did you not know?"

The dowager gave her a remote smile. "I am afraid not But then, I scarcely know any of the parties involved."

Robert gave a quick glance in Lady Maude's direction. Any blush that might have stained her cheeks had fled. Her face was now a ghastly white.

I am damned if I am going to ask for the hand of a girl who loves another, he thought *Let her take some other fool to husband. Enough of listening to my mother. The girl that I marry will have to love me as profoundly as I love her.* He took a handkerchief to his brow. It had been a very narrow escape.

In the still of night, when the bustle of the castle had died down, he sat in his library, sipping a glass of brandy, and wondering if there was anyone in the whole of England he could love with his heart and soul. It was not his first glass of the amber liquid, and at that point he was about ready to laugh at his own folly. *That's it*, he thought, *drink your bloody self to oblivion—perhaps you will get a good night's sleep, for a change.*

There was a gentle rapping on the door. "Go away, whoever you are." This was followed by a hiccough. He suddenly became aware that Lady Maude stood before him, clad in a dressing gown. With her hair hanging loose about her shoulders she was a very beguiling sight illuminated in the candlelight.

"Go to bed, little girl, before we do something we both shall be sorry for."

"Robert, you are foxed."

It occurred to him that she chose a fine time to get familiar.

"I have come to tell you that I am prepared to marry you."

This intelligence sobered him immediately and he bolted from his chair. "It would be politic to wait until you are asked. Why should I marry a young lady who wears her heart on her sleeve for another?"

"I declare, I do not know what you are talking about." Maude looked as if she was about to faint.

"I think you do, Lady Maude. It would be less embarrassing all around if we were to continue as if nothing has happened, and then at the end of the week, you may tell your worthy brother that you rejected my suit."

She backed away from him, stumbling over a footstool in the process. He gave her a steadying arm.

She brushed him away. "I do not know what you mean. In any case, I think you are perfectly horrid and I would not dream of marrying you."

"Bravo, young lady." A round of applause accompanied

this remark. "I admire your style, but must confess I find your behavior totally baffling. After those kisses we shared, I fail to see how you could love another."

"You and I have never kissed. The very idea!"

"Of course we have. I shall never forget that day in the rose arbor. You looked so delectable in the blue dress with the violets nestled beneath your lovely bosom, I could not help but kiss you."

She gave him a look of wide-eyed amazement. In spite of what had transpired earlier in the evening, he thought she looked rather lovely at that moment with the candlelight turning her knee-length hair to flames.

With lust replacing common sense, he took her in his arms and kissed her. Profound disappointment quickly followed on the heels of base desire, and he gently pushed her away. "I am afraid kissing you is not the same heady experience I remember, my lady. You, too, must have noticed the magic has gone. Perhaps it was the blue dress."

Maude gave her head an angry toss. "And perhaps, Your Grace, the drink has addled your brain. You see, I do not own a blue dress." Her hand flew to her mouth. "Oh dear. You did mention violets?"

"I shall never forget them."

"No wonder poor Lucy has become downright dowdy. You dreadful man, she is terrified you will recognize her and kiss her again."

"Yes," he said dryly. "I can see how any right-thinking young lady would consider it a fate worse than death."

Then her words sunk in. "Wait. Did you just say that it was *Lucy* I kissed in the rose arbor?"

"I rather expect so."

He sank back into his chair with a groan. "Return to your bed and leave me to drink my brandy in peace. You have just told me that I am in love with the veriest bluestocking in all of England. Nay. In the whole world, I am willing to wager. I am afraid that that is going to take quite a bit of getting used to."

Eleven

After considerable tossing and turning, Lucy had finally dropped off to sleep when she was rudely awakened by a vigorous shake. She opened her eyes to find Maude peering over her, her face illuminated by the light of a double-sconced candlestick she held in her hand.

Lucy sat up and rubbed her eyes. "Maude? Is there something amiss?"

Maude placed the candlestick on the nightstand and crawled into Lucy's bed. "Brr! That is better. Why is it the larger the house, the colder the drafts?"

"Maude, why are you roaming around at this late hour? Were you having a bad dream?"

Maude sighed. "Oh, Lucy, I suppose one could say that, only, unfortunately, I happened to be awake at the time."

A log sputtered in the grate and flared into flame, illuminating the bedchamber in a rosy glow. Lucy got out of bed and banked the fire with more wood. "Please continue," she said, then attempted to coax the fire back to life with several jabs of a poker.

"I am afraid I have made a complete cake of myself."

Lucy replaced the poker and turned to face Maude. "That is not true. Everyone liked your singing this evening."

"My singing?" Maude burst out laughing. It was a hollow sound. "Would that were all I had to live down."

There was a catch in her voice and Lucy hastened back into the bed to console her. "There, there. I am sure you are making far too much of this. There is nothing you could do to warrant such distress."

Maude groaned. "Would that include bursting into a

gentleman's library and informing him that I am willing to marry him?"

Lucy's gasped. "Maude! Why did you not wait to be asked?"

"What a coincidence, His Grace wondered the same thing."

"How unchivalrous. Would you want to marry a man who shows so little regard for your feelings?"

"That is no longer a consideration. His Grace made it very clear he did not wish to marry me. It seems he is in love with someone else."

"Are you sure? Then why did he go to the trouble to ask for your hand?"

"That was before he realized I was in love with Harcourt."

"Harcourt?"

"Viscount Langley." Maude looked wry. "I gave myself away when hearing of the viscount's forthcoming nuptials. It seems I am not very good at hiding my feelings."

She put her hand over Lucy's. "You, on the other hand, are very adept at such. Dear, dear Lucy, why did you not tell me that cad kissed you in the rose arbor? It must have been most distressing."

Lucy's mind began to race. He knew. He knew! *Oh, my heavens, he knew it was I, in the rose arbor. What pleasure he must have derived from my discomfort. How amusing it must have been for him. As Maude once remarked of the man, rather like a cat toying with a helpless mouse. What made me think he possessed one shred of sincerity? Those kisses meant nothing to him. Yet when his lips touched mine ...*

Maude shook her by the shoulder. "Lucy? Please forgive me, I should not have been so blunt in the telling. He upset me so much I did not stop to consider how this news might affect you."

"H—he told you he kissed me?" Lucy's voice broke. "I—I wonder how many others he might have told? It must have made for high amusement at all the gentlemen's clubs."

Maude clasped her by the shoulders. "Dismiss such thoughts from your head. The Duke of Linborough is a very proud gentleman and would do nothing so ignoble. Besides, he was unaware that it was *you* he kissed in the rose arbor, until I told him. That is the only comfort I derive from my own gaffe. He is too much of a gentleman to betray either one of us."

"You knew he kissed me? But how? And what possessed you to tell His Grace?" Lucy felt a mixture of resentment to what she perceived as betrayal by Maude and relief that the duke was innocent of such perfidy.

"I did not mean to. The subject would not have arisen, if he had not taken the liberty of kissing me."

"H—he *kissed* you? After spurning your offer of marriage? How odd."

"Yes, it was. I got the impression it was an act of desperation, rather than passion. He took no pleasure in the doing."

"Do not take it as a personal affront, Maude dear. His Grace must be one of those mad dukes one hears about"

Maude giggled. "Of course. Otherwise he would have found me absolutely irresistible."

"Or perhaps gentlemen find the kisses of other ladies abhorrent once they fall in love. I wonder who she could be?"

"Who?"

"The lady who has his heart."

"For a girl who is so terribly clever, you can be incredibly dense. It is you, Lucy Garwood. Have I not been telling you this? His Grace is in love with you."

He loves me! Lucy's heart soared with joy only to come crashing down to the depths of despair.

"Maude, I am so terribly sorry. I thought if I were to keep quiet, His Grace would be non the wiser and would marry you— if that is what you wanted."

"Do not shoulder a blame that is not yours, Lucy. His Grace spurned my offer of marriage because he knew my love did not go with it. He is well aware of my misguided regard for that treacherous toad, Viscount Langley."

"After his perfidy you still harbor a *tendre* for the gentleman?"

"Alas, I have no say in the matter. As I once pointed out to James when he was not treating Emily as well as he should, true love is unconditional."

Lucy patted Maude's cheek. "I think in many ways, sweet

friend, you are the wisest person I know. You certainly have a most generous spirit. Many a girl would have not delved any deeper and have blamed me for what happened."

She smiled, but Lucy could see that holding back the tears was an effort. "Then many a girl would have been wrong," Maude rejoined. "Robert Renquist can no more help loving Lucy Garwood, than I can help loving Harcourt Langley.

"Even if he had accepted my shameful offer of marriage, I doubt we would have followed through. In this, His Grace and I are in complete agreement; a marriage should be based on true love."

Maude leaned forward and dug her elbows in the counterpane. "However, that does not mean that I forgive him for the rebuff."

"No?"

"Absolutely not. That might take years."

"Years?"

"Eons. How dare he reject me? Who does he think he is?"

"The most top-lofty duke in all of England?"

They both flopped back against their pillows and giggled, glad to find humor, however remote, in the situation.

When their laughter subsided, Maude added, "His rejection of me was the least of it. How *dare* he not find pleasure in kissing me?" The humor fled from her voice. "Lucy, do you suppose I just do not have it in me to kiss well? What if every would-be suitor were to steal a kiss from me, only to go howling into the night? In which case, I should end up being the most oft-kissed, loneliest old maid society has ever known."

"Nonsense, Maude. When the right gentleman kisses you, everything else will fall into place."

"Is that how it was when His Grace kissed you?"

"I felt it all the way down to my toes."

Maude's eyes widened. "Really?

Lucy nodded.

Maude sighed. "His Grace implied that he felt that way too—about kissing you—that is. But suppose kissing is a special talent, like dancing, or singing? Those are also things you do so much better than I."

"You have nothing to fear, Maude. When the right gentleman comes along…"

"But how can you know this?"

"Because I kissed someone else, to make sure."

"Lucy! Surely not?"

"Alas, I wish I could say otherwise."

"But who? You rarely put in an appearance at our 'at homes.'" She grabbed Lucy's arm. "It was Miles. It had to be." She giggled. "How did you go about it? Did you ask him to kiss you? Or did you just boldly walk up to him and steal a kiss? Either way, I expect the poor chap was shocked to the very core of his being. He is very protective of us Garwood girls."

"Yes, it was Miles, and I had the devil's own time convincing him to cooperate in the experiment."

"You *told* him it was an experiment?"

"But of course. I did not want him to think otherwise—it would not have been fair to lead him on."

"Oh, quite." This remark was followed by a gurgle of laughter.

"Maude! I fail to see the humor in this. It was important for me to know if kissing one man was any different from kissing another."

"Lucy. That is shocking. One cannot go about kissing gentlemen right and left to see if they will suit"

"It will not be necessary. Kissing Miles made me realize that His Grace spoke the truth. When we kissed, something wonderful happened. Miles's kisses were merely pleasant. Since marriage to the Duke of Linborough is out of the question, I daresay I shall never kiss another gentleman as long as I live." She wiped away a tear with the sleeve of her night rail.

Maude clucked sympathetically. "Dear, dear Lucy, let your tears flow, you are entitled to them. I am not the brightest of people, but even *I* realize that there is something wrong with a society that arranges marriages for their children predicated on rank and fortune, rather than love. To my way of thinking, you are far too good for His Grace. It is hardly likely that he will marry you, so serve him right if he fails to find happiness with anyone else."

Lucy clasped Maude's hand. "I know you say that out of loyalty to me, but do not even think such a thing. I only wish for that dear, dear gentleman all that is good in life."

"Dear, dear gentleman? Darling Lucy, you are living proof that love is indeed blind."

In spite of a pounding head, Robert rose early the next morning and forswore breakfast in favor of a walk along the cliffs. He was in no mood to engage any of his guests in small talk—especially that little minx, Lady Maude. The very idea, barging in on a chap like that with an offer of marriage, all the time pining for that young puppy, Langley!

All the same, he had to admit that there was an element of humor in the whole thing. Not unlike a Shakespeare comedy of errors, only without the heroine running about in doublet and hose, but rather hiding behind a mousy demeanor. What an odd thing to do. If only to make him suffer the more, most girls would have gone out of their way to look their loveliest—even if a gentleman's advances were not welcomed.

He recalled a dark-haired beauty he had taken as a mistress, who, when she decided to leave him in favor of a protector who offered her a more fun-filled life, had never looked lovelier than when bidding him a last farewell. He smiled grimly. She had been such a captivating little jade.

As he contemplated the episode, he glanced down at the thin strip of beach that had appeared at the early morning ebb tide and was surprised to see Lucy come around an outcropping of rocks. His glance then went to the steps hewn out of the side of the cliffs—surely she had not braved such a descent? Many a man had balked at the idea.

He followed her down at a speed most would have considered suicidal, but the repetition of years stood behind the doing. On reaching the beach, he stopped for a moment to catch his breath. He saw her stoop down to remove her shoes and stockings, then enter the water to traverse a group of rocks jutting into the lapping waves.

"The girl is too foolhardy to be let out on her own," he muttered. "She has no sense of danger whatsoever." To his surprise, he found he had mixed feelings about her lack of caution. Part of him wanted to shake her until her teeth rattled; a softer side wanted to watch over her and keep her safe.

He observed her progress around the rocks, one arm outstretched in an attempt to maintain her balance, while she used her other hand to hold her skirts out of the water. He had imagined her limbs to be skinny and lacking in curves, but his view of her afforded him the delectable sight of slender calves and even a glimpse of a firm, creamy thigh. His heart beat faster.

Then his concern for her safety had a cooling effect on his ardor. *I was right. The foolish girl bears constant watching. The very idea, exposing herself in such a manner. Anyone could be lurking around the other side of those rocks, just waiting to ravish her.*

Even as he grumbled over the matter, he realized the only one who presented any danger to her was he. This fact left him much to ponder. She was not the sort of girl who usually stirred his passion. He had thought her figure to be too slender for his taste, her hips too narrow, but after gazing at those long, shapely legs...

His reverie was broken by the sound of a sharp little scream, followed by a splash of water. He raced along the beach and without stopping to remove his boots, rushed into the waves at the point where they broke over the rocks.

By the time he caught up with Lucy, she was making her way to shore, soaked from head to toe, the hem of her dress trailing in the water. She turned as he approached and gave him a woeful look.

"Is it not enough that I have made a cake of myself without you, of all people, turning up to witness my humility?"

Far from looking humble, Robert thought she looked like a magnificent sea nymph newly risen out of the ocean. Her clothes clung to her, revealing that despite her slender frame, her bosom was shapely, and her waist slender, rendering a delicious curve to hips which heretofore he had considered to be nonexistent.

As he beheld her wondrous form, a lump came into his

throat. He wanted her so badly he ached to the very depths of his soul. Then he saw the distress in her tawny eyes and knew that above all, he wanted to love and to cherish her for the rest of his days.

She put her hands on her hips and glared at him. "Go ahead. Laugh if it will make you happy. I know you despise and pity me for being, heaven forfend, that dreaded anathema, a female with a brain, and what is worse, one who does not even have the good sense to hide the fact."

As she spoke she started to shiver. At first Robert thought it was out of anger, then he realized she was trembling because of her wet clothes. He took off his jacket and put it on her.

"Have you quite finished, Miss Garwood? Or would you like to take a riding crop to my shoulders? I have seen wet hens calmer than you."

Her lower lip began to quiver. "I beg your pardon, Your Grace, for a moment there I quite forgot myself."

He buttoned the coat, and held her close. "It is I who should be apologizing to you. You have no idea what you do to me—or of the things I would like to do to you. This for instance." He showered her face with kisses. It tasted of salt. "I have dreamed of nothing else since that morning among the roses."

He pulled back and searched her face. "Have you any idea how beautiful you are? No, I suppose not. You are no coquette." He sought her lips, but she turned her head aside.

"*Please*, Your Grace?"

"Call me Robert. I intend to call you Lucinda."

"I prefer Lucy. Lucy, plain and simple. But if you have any regard for my reputation, please continue to call me Miss Garwood."

He pulled her closer to him. "Have any regard for your reputation? Darling girl. I want to make you my wife."

Her eyes filled with tears. "Alas, Your Grace, my life must take another path."

He let her go. "I am assuming that Lord Northwycke is your guardian? Otherwise you would have returned to your parents long ago. Are they abroad?"

Lucy shook her head. "My parents died almost two years ago. Cousin James was kind enough to take me in. So you see, it would not be the thing to bring shame down upon him, in any shape or form."

Robert kissed the tip of her nose. "Dear, sweet Lucy, you do not have it in you to dishonor anyone."

Her lips parted as if to protest the statement and Robert took the opportunity to plunder their sweet essence. A tiny moan sounded in her throat, and then she pushed him away.

"This will not do, Your Grace. No, not at all."

Robert acquiesced. "You are quite right I shall follow your rules for the present, even to calling you Miss Garwood, when I want the whole world to know how I feel about you. Right now, I think we had better get you back to the castle as soon as possible."

She nodded, her whole frame shivering with cold.

He carried her around the rocks, then made her sit on one of the smoother ones while he helped her into her stockings and half boots, which lay discarded in the sand. By now, her teeth were chattering and she offered no resistance to his ministrations.

As he pushed her foot into a boot, he gazed up at her face. Her lips had turned blue and she looked perfectly wretched.

"Whatever possessed you to embark on this foolhardy endeavor all by yourself?" he asked. "You could have drowned, fallen down those steps—or even worse, encountered smugglers who would have been only too eager to rob you of your innocence."

He did not expect her to answer, nor did she. He put a protective arm around her shoulders and helped her to the cliff. "Do not panic, and do exactly as I say, and in no time at all you will be thawing out in a nice, hot bath."

The return trip up the cliff was an arduous one. The only words Robert uttered the whole time were ones of caution and encouragement. He knew by her weakened state that she never would have made it alone. Fear pricked his scalp at the very thought. *Once she is in my care*, he thought, *I will see to it that she is never again exposed to such risk. What could she have been thinking?*

There was no doubt in his mind that she would be his to care for. Regardless of what plans had been made for Lucy's future, what guardian would pass up the chance to make her a duchess? He decided it would be prudent to let a decent interval elapse before approaching James Garwood on the subject. Things would certainly go easier if perhaps in the interim, Lady Maude were to accept an offer of marriage from another suitor.

Their return to the confines of the castle generated a flurry of activity. Amid calls for a hot bath to be prepared for Miss Garwood, Robert could not help but notice the look of censure Geraldine Garwood accorded Lucy.

"As soon as you have changed your clothes, young lady, I should like to talk to you." The dowager's tone was forbidding.

Robert felt sorry for Lucy. Things did not bode well for her. Lucy seemed well aware of this, for she looked very forlorn as she made her way to her chamber. It made him all the more determined to love and protect her.

"Darling Lucy," he murmured under his breath, "when you become my wife, no one will *dare* to use you so."

Twelve

Lucy gazed steadfastly out the carriage window in a vain attempt to distance herself from the drama unfolding around her. She saw James rein in Tarquin in order for the carriage to catch up with him.

"Maude, how could you? If you could only give me one good reason for such irrational behavior, I would try to understand."

Her mother had repeated versions of this diatribe for the past two hours, while Maude just stared ahead in stony-faced silence. Beneath the folds of their traveling dresses Lucy gave Maude's hand a sympathetic squeeze. Maude shot her a grateful smile.

"I am glad you find this amusing, you ungrateful little horror."

Maude covered her ears with her hands. "For pity's sake, Mama, please stop."

For a moment, her mother just stared at her in openmouthed surprise, and then, with eyes blazing, she leaned over and tapped her shoulder with her lorgnette. Maude recoiled, then broke into tears. These quickly dissolved into what Lucy perceived to be a fit of righteous anger.

"You want a good excuse, Mama? You shall have one. I shall not be marrying the Duke of Linborough because he did not ask me."

Lucy held her breath, waiting for the carriage roof to fall in. An occurrence that was not too long in the coming.

"What did you say?" The dowager almost lost her balance in an effort to grab Maude by the shoulders. "How dare you compound your perfidy with such a falsehood?" She proceeded to give Maude a vigorous shaking.

Lucy threw caution to the wind and put a restraining hand on her arm. "Please, your ladyship, before you hurt her. Maude speaks the truth."

Lady Northwycke glared at Lucy. "I would not be in the least surprised if *your* disgraceful behavior has some bearing on His Grace's repudiation of Maude."

She turned to Maude. "I only want what is best for you." She bit her lip and gazed distractedly out the carriage window.

"I know that, Mama. This must be most distressing for you."

Her mother puffed up like a barnyard foul ready to protect her chick. "Distressing for me? How dare that odious man treat you so? The very *idea* of inviting us to Linborough under the pretext of asking for your hand, and then not following through. What must he have been thinking? I would not be in the least surprised if your brother were to call him out." Her hands clenched. "If I were a man he would certainly live to regret this."

"Do not upset yourself over it, Mama. His Grace was well within his rights to withdraw his suit, and it had nothing to do with Lucy falling into the ocean. You see, he is one of those strange gentlemen who believes in marrying for love."

Lady Northwycke's eyes widened. "Marrying for love? How odd—but then, his father did that—and look what a pickle that landed him in. It is said the poor man never knew another moment's peace until the day he died."

Lucy gave Maude a relieved smile. Seemingly her friend had survived the situation relatively unscathed. Lady Northwycke lost no time in ridding her of such a fond illusion.

She leaned over and placed a heavy hand on Maude's knee. "One moment, miss. From this, one must deduce that His Grace carried a *tendre* for you. Would you mind telling me what you said to him that would cause him to change his mind?"

Maude sighed, a look of resignation on her face. "I suppose it would come to light sooner or later, as His Grace remarked, I am not good at hiding my emotions."

"Oh? Pray continue."

Lucy cringed. Her ladyship's words crackled with frost.

"When it was mentioned during the course of conversation

115

that Viscount Langley was about to announce his betrothal to a Scottish lady, His Grace happened to be paying close attention to my reaction to the news. I rather think it was not by accident that he did so—the gentleman is not a fool."

"But evidently you are. Maude. Maude. When are you going to grow up? You have lost everything for a scapegrace who is not worthy to tie your shoelaces."

Maude's head drooped. "I am well aware of that, Mama. I did not ask to fall in love with him. Viscount Langley is probably betrothed to his Scottish sweetheart by now." She gave a little sob. "I expect his attentions toward me were merely a means of passing the time until he could return to Scotland. Tell me, Mama, why are gentlemen so horrid? Is there not one out there who would consider me worthy of his regard?"

Her mother's expression softened. "There, there, my little dove. You are a most beautiful young lady, not only in appearance but also in disposition. No one has a kinder heart than you, my daughter."

"Do you really think so?"

"Without a doubt. A gentleman worthy of your regard will one day show up at our door, and all of this will fade away like an inconsequential dream."

"Oh, Mama, I do love you so."

Maude moved to sit next to her mother, who lost no time in putting a comforting arm around her little ewe lamb. They stayed in that position until they came to the inn where they would spend the night.

Later that evening, the four of them gathered in Lady Northwycke's room in front of a cosy fire. She had been assigned the best room the establishment had to offer. It was no better or worse than any other accommodations one might receive while on a journey—in other words woefully lacking in the comforts a lady of quality might consider her due.

With her arm around Maude's shoulder, she gave James an account of her fall from grace. "So, you see, that is why he did not offer for her."

James shrugged. "I gathered as much. The situation being

what it is, I believe it is all for the better."

"For the better? How can you adopt such a cavalier attitude? I swear, both of my children are quite mad."

"Maude would not have been happy in a loveless marriage, would you, dear?"

Lucy held her breath at the sign of displeasure that flashed across the dowager's face. "Then for heaven's sake, why did you drag us all the way to that dreadful place and make me suffer the company of Martha Rowebotham."

"Rawbottom?"

On hearing this name, Lucy had a hard time keeping a straight face.

Lady Northwycke looked exasperated. "It is spelled R-o-w-e-b-o-t-h-a-m, as well you know. There are enough upstarts from Lancashire invading polite society, flaunting the money they have made in the cotton mills, for you to be aware of that."

"Only our friend the duchess was not quite so fortunate," Robert inserted.

"I am sure she would rather spring from the genteel poverty of the clergy, rather than be termed a mushroom." Lady Northwycke punctuated this remark with a sniff that no amount of words could have equaled.

James smiled. "Aptly put, but we digress."

"Digress?"

"You questioned my doubting the wisdom of Maude marrying the son of the aforementioned Martha Rowebotham."

"I would prefer to *die* than marry that odious creature!" Maude declared.

Lady Northwycke waved her down. "Hush, child. I am speaking to your brother." She turned to him. "I think I deserve an answer. Your ill-considered act has caused your sister a great deal of grief."

James gave her shoulder the briefest of touches. "And for that, I am truly sorry. You see I suspect that His Grace is capable of deep love for the woman he would make his duchess. In this I expect he takes after his father."

She rolled her eyes. "Come now, James."

James shrugged. "I know you do not believe such a union is possible, neither did I, until I met my darling Emily. I just thought with close propinquity Maude might grow to feel the same about His Grace. Is it so wrong to wish that sort of happiness for one's sister?"

Lady Northwycke sighed. "I expect not. It seems that all the old traditions are falling by the wayside."

"I think that under the circumstances we shall not be returning to London. I rather believe Maude has taken all the courtships she can handle for one Season," James said.

"I heartily agree," Maude declared.

"I also," her mother added. "Men are such brutes."

"I say, that is a bit thick, Mother."

She rose, her nostrils pinched so close together they turned white. "I misstate the situation by half." She gave Maude's shoulder a motherly squeeze. "At least this enables me to keep my baby by my side for at least one more Season."

James also rose and kissed her cheek. "You see, Mother, there is a bright side to all of this."

She tapped his shoulder with her lorgnette. "That does not mitigate your hand in these proceedings."

"Nor for a moment did I entertain such a notion." He consulted his fob watch. "Seven of the clock. If we wish to get a decent meal, we had better make our way into the room the innkeeper set aside for our use."

"Decent meal? I recognize the odor of old mutton boiling in a cauldron when I smell it. One can only hope it was slaughtered for the occasion, and not carrion plucked from the downs."

Lucy and Maude looked at each other and grimaced.

"And a hearty appetite to you also, Mother dear," James said.

The Duchess of Linborough was in a very bad mood, and had been ever since waving good-bye to the Garwood entourage. Nothing seemed to suit her—from the way her luckless abigail dressed her hair, to the food their cook prepared for the table.

She snapped once too often at Robert and finally his

patience wore thin. "For pity's sake, Mother, the sooner you become reconciled to the fact that I have no intention of marrying Lady Maude, the better it will be for all concerned."

"Would you mind telling me why? I have never felt so mortified. I half expected Northwycke to call you out on the matter."

"I doubt the gentleman would involve his sister in such a scandal. As to why? Call me persnickety, if you will, but I refuse to marry a lady who is in love with another man."

Her Grace's china blue eyes widened in disbelief. "Surely she did not admit to such perfidy?"

"She did not have to. When the subject of Viscount Langley's forthcoming betrothal arose the other evening, the most stricken expression came over her face."

"She favors a viscount over a duke? And one that does not return her regard, to boot? You have had a narrow escape—the girl is obviously quite mad." She gave her coiffure a pat and smiled like a cat that has beaten all the other barnyard tabbies to the cream. "Of course, her mother is to blame. The woman has not the faintest notion of rearing a young girl."

Try as he might, Robert could not resist ruining her moment. "Then I suppose the same could be said for the Shrewsbury Garwoods."

Her smug demeanor was replaced by a frown. "What on earth are you talking about, Robert? You know how I detest riddles."

"Merely that Miss Lucy Garwood also did not regard me as prime husband material. She lost no time in spurning my advances."

The duchess popped out of her chair. "You spoke for *that* scrap of humanity? For heaven's sake—*why?* She possesses not one shred of feminine charm."

"Admittedly, most of the time she manages to hide her allure very well, but rest assured, Mother, the girl is an extraordinary beauty."

She plopped back into her chair. "And to think I had the temerity to question Geraldine Garwood's fitness as a mother.

Robert, I fear that not only are you ripe for Bedlam, but you are going blind, to boot."

"Be that as it may, she turned me down in spite of the fact that I have reason to believe that she returns my love."

"How could you possibly know that?"

"Kisses do not lie."

"Good heavens. Pray do not tell me you have been gamboling among the Garwood maidens like a moonstruck satyr? If it should get back to the marquess, you would not live long enough to marry either one of them."

"I am well aware of that, Mother. In a way, this whole silly charade can be laid at your door."

The duchess glared at him. "Right Blame your poor mother. You sound more like your father every day." She clutched her bosom. "No one could possibly comprehend the indignities I have been made to suffer."

"I do not recall Father ever saying boo to a goose."

"Oh. So I am a goose, now? When I think of the agony I went through to bring you into the world…" She dabbed at an imaginary tear with a handkerchief she kept in her reticule for just such a purpose.

Robert knew when to back down. "You read too much into what I said. I merely meant that if you had not put the idea into my head, I would not have kissed Miss Garwood and thereby fallen under her spell."

The duchess bristled. "Now I know you are mad. I never suggested you should kiss that little mouse."

"No, you did not. But when I did so, I was under the impression that she was Lady Maude—she looked particularly beautiful that morning. I did not discover my mistake until I kissed Lady Maude a couple of days ago—I assure you, it was not the same."

She looked mystified. "What on earth would possess an antidote like Miss Garwood to spurn an offer of marriage from a man every other girl is scrambling to marry?"

"She mumbled something about having to follow another path, but even as she uttered the words there were tears in her eyes."

"She has most likely been promised to one of her whey-faced cousins. The Shrewsbury Garwoods are as rich as Croesus and are not known for dissipating their wealth by marrying outsiders. Let her go, Robert. They may have the blood of three royal dynasties flowing in their veins, but no good can come of marrying into such a brood."

"Mother, if you studied the bloodlines of horses with half the enthusiasm you apply to those of the *ton*, you could own the finest stables in England."

"I shall ignore that piece of impertinence. You may be head of our family, but I am still your mother."

"You are quite right. Please accept my apology."

She patted his hand. "I know you did not mean it, Robert dear. The last couple of weeks must have been a strain. I think we should sever all connections with that dreadful family."

"I am sorry to disappoint you, Mother, but I am afraid that I cannot make such a promise. When the time is right, I shall do everything in my power to make Lucinda Garwood the next Duchess of Linborough."

She looked astounded. "Oh my word. Where did I go wrong? I do believe you will pursue this folly to the point of madness."

He smiled grimly. "And beyond."

For once, his mother had no rejoinder.

Thirteen

The family's return to Northwycke Hall did not even elicit a raised brow from Hobbes. Since Emily was in residence, the household was functioning as usual. Chambermaids were sent to air out Lucy's and James's rooms and to put fresh linens on their beds. Otherwise, it was as if they had never left.

Maude and her mother stayed long enough to partake of refreshments with Emily, and to coo over James Elias. In the meantime, word of their mistress's return was sent over to the Dower House, so dustsheets could be removed from the furniture and the rooms aired out.

The following morning, a servant was sent to London by carriage, to pick up the rest of the family's personal effects. Because of this, when Viscount Langley called to visit Maude, later in the week, one of the Mayfair servants was able to tell him that she had returned to the country.

A day later, Viscount Langley stood on the doorstep of Northwycke Hall, seeking permission from James to ask Maude to marry him. Dinner at Northwycke Hall that evening was a very festive affair. Amid the gaiety, the newly engaged couple were toasted at every remove of a course. By the time they were down to the sweeter wines, they had all lost a considerable amount of their English reserve.

When the meal came to an end, Harcourt rose to his feet "I wish to make a toast to James. Although he made it perfectly clear that I am unworthy of the honor, he nevertheless gave his permission for me to ask his beautiful sister for her hand in marriage." He raised his glass. "To my future brother-in-law, James, who has my undying gratitude."

After they were seated once more, Emily turned to James.

"Surely Harcourt jests? Please tell me you did not say such a dreadful thing."

James grinned. "I most certainly did. I thought to tease him a little before giving him leave to propose to Maude. He fails to mention that I also ventured the opinion that all we gentlemen are unworthy of the love of the innocent little darlings we take to wife."

This remark inspired a round of laughter. When it had died down, Emily said, "If ever you decide to be horrid to me, I shall bring up the matter of your unworthiness."

James kissed her hand. "How could anyone be horrid to you, my dearest Emily?"

Lucy had remained subdued for most of the meal. It was Maude's day, and she did not want to take any of the attention away from her friend, but she had a very clear picture of what had taken place between James and Harcourt, and it made her giggle.

She became aware that she had everyone's undivided attention. "Forgive me," she said, "but I should have liked to have seen Harcourt's face when he thought his hopes of marrying Maude were completely dashed."

"Then, Lucy, one must deduce that you enjoy tragedies," Harcourt replied, "for I declare, I had half a mind to throw myself into the lake."

"Harcourt, you exaggerate," James inserted. "You indulged in a great deal of cravat-clutching, nothing more."

The dowager looked reproachful. "It appears to me, James, that you treated poor Harcourt shamefully."

Harcourt raised his hand. "Wait. There is more."

Maude gave her brother a look. "What more could you possibly do to him? I do not understand, James. This is not like you at all."

"He suggested I would have a better chance of your accepting my suit if I were to plead my case in the Dower House arbor."

James shrugged. "It was said in good faith, Harcourt old chap. Young girls love romantic settings, and I wanted you to have every possible chance to secure a happy outcome. What ensued was of your own doing."

As if on cue, the Garwood ladies turned expectant faces in Harcourt's direction. "Do not believe a word of it I merely supposed that the arbor had white roses, for your family seems to have a fondness for them, and James brought about my head such a ludicrous story about an ancestor of yours I cannot believe I was gullible enough to swallow it."

"You mean the one about Great-Great-Grandmother Eulalie?" Maude asked.

Harcourt looked puzzled. "You mean James spoke the truth?"

"Absolutely. Eulalie was of the opinion that young ladies were more inclined to accept wedding proposals in settings that did not clash with their pretty dresses. White roses meet this requirement do you not agree?"

Harcourt grinned. "It seemed the sort of thing that would appeal to the gentler sex. Your sensibilities are far more refined than ours." He squeezed Maude's hand. "I needed all the confidence I could garner to ask this dear girl to be my wife, so I was willing to grasp at anything that might help me."

"Even to relying on white roses to achieve your goal?" James interjected.

"Yes," said Harcourt. "Even that. So imagine my dismay, when you informed me that the Dower House arbor is noted for the particularly lush quality of its—" Here the rest of them jumped in and chorused, "*wisteria!*"

They all laughed, but none heartier than Maude's betrothed did.

"Welcome to the family, Harcourt." James said. "You are a good sport for putting up with our nonsense."

"There is even a better reason for welcoming Harcourt into our midst," Lucy interjected.

"And what would that be?" James responded.

"He and Maude are a perfect match."

Lucy firmly believed this. The longer she had been acquainted with him, the surer she had become of it.

"Hear! Hear!" the rest of the Garwoods replied.

• • •

The morning after Maude and Harcourt became engaged, Lucy skipped breakfast and made her way to the stables. Since becoming a member of the family, she had become, if not as proficient a horsewoman as Maude, at least a tolerable one.

James had given her a horse, a gentle dappled mare she had promptly named Daisy, after the sway-backed old wreck who had faithfully pulled her father's rag-and-bone cart around London for as long as she could remember. James had told her Daisy was hers to keep. It did not take long for the animal to steal her heart away.

She arrived at the paddock to find Mickey currying Tarquin. The horse's coat gleamed like burnished copper from all the attention. Mickey shot her a smile.

"Come to ride Daisy, 'ave you?"

Lucy nodded.

"You'll be lucky if she'll give you the time of day. Leaving 'er so long."

"I have been to visit her. I have not had time to ride her. Things have been at sixes and sevens at the Hall".

Mickey raised the brush from Tarquin's flank. "So I've 'eard. Lady Maude spoken for, is she?"

Lucy smiled. "I see the footmen lost no time in spreading the news."

"Everyone 'as—'cept for Mr. 'obbes, and 'e wouldn't open his gob if they tore 'im limb from limb."

Lucy laughed. "It is a matter of professional pride on his part I understand there has been a Hobbes serving as butler at Northwycke for many generations. In fact, one of them actually did sacrifice himself to save the family from the Roundheads."

"Criminy. I was only joking. I would say there's more to an 'obbes than meets the eye."

He gave Tarquin one more going over with the brush. "There you are, my 'andsome lad." He turned to Lucy. "'E fair preens after I've done with 'im. Very vain is our Tarquin."

"So he should be. You do a marvelous job, Mickey."

Mickey blossomed with the praise. "I'll 'ave Daisy ready for you in a jiffy. Going over to the kiddies' place, are you?"

"Yes. I just hated being away from the children, but his lordship would not hear of my staying home. I cannot imagine why. My attendance at Linborough Castle served no useful purpose."

"I am thinking that was not 'is lordship's reason for taking you there."

"What do you mean?"

"The way I see it, 'e was looking after your interests, young Lucy."

"Oh? In what way?"

"Being a guest of someone as top-lofty as the duke raises your standing, gives you consequence, as the gentry says. No doubt trying to improve your chances when it's your turn to be married."

"Then he was wasting his time, for I doubt I shall ever marry."

"Whoa there. One o' them young bloods tried to trifle with you, 'as he?" His fist curled up. "Just say the word, and 'is sparking days are over."

"*Please*, Mickey. You know I would not allow that to happen. I have seen too many girls dragged down into the gutter by such folly."

As she rode over the rise to Hope House, she told herself that she was not as sensible as she would have Mickey believe.

"It is fortunate that Robert Renquist is an honorable man," she muttered to herself. "If he were not, I should imagine I would be very easy prey. I was half seduced just by the passionate looks he gave me."

She had made the trip so often Daisy needed no urging on the downward path to Hope House. Lucy viewed the rooftop displayed below. Chimneys adorned it like a crop of odd-looking toadstools. From the very first time she had beheld the old manor house, she thought it belonged in a whimsical fairytale involving goblins and fairy godmothers.

A fairy godmother would serve me in good stead this very moment, she thought She patted the mare's head. "You see, Daisy, with one wave of her magic wand she could make me a lady with an impeccable background, and I could marry my duke and be happy, just like dear, sweet Maude is with her viscount. But perhaps Maude is more deserving than I am. Heaven knows, she has a far sunnier nature."

Daisy whickered.

"You do not have to be so quick to agree, you wretched horse. Nevertheless, it is a point to ponder. I may not have it in me to make any man happy, much less one so complicated as Robert Renquist. It is probably far better that I remain a spinster."

Even as she spoke the words, she experienced a longing to be in her beloved's arms and to have his lips showering her face with kisses. She thought it amazing that such firmly set lips could be so soft, when touching hers....

As she climbed the stairs to the nursery, the sound of a child in the throes of a temper tantrum pushed the bittersweet thoughts of love aside. Lucy recognized the lusty lung power of William, the offspring of one of the chambermaids of Northwycke Hall who had died giving birth to him.

His father, who had forced himself upon the hapless girl and several others as well, had been sent to a penal colony in Australia for his perfidy. There were those in the village who were of the opinion that even hanging was too good for him, and that he had been let off too lightly. Listening to the sobs of the motherless child, Lucy was inclined to agree.

She entered the nursery to a scene fraught with misery. William, a large child for a toddler, lay on the well-scrubbed boards of the floor, rigid with rage. The nursemaid, Lizzie, who did not look a day over thirteen, hovered over him, tears of frustration pooling in her eyes. A solemn little girl watched in wide-eyed silence, her thumb firmly placed in her mouth.

A look of relief crossed Lizzie's face when Lucy entered the room.

"Thank heaven you've come back, Miss. William has been a holy horror from the moment you left."

Lucy sighed. "So it would seem." She scanned the room. "Where is Nurse Wilcox? You should not be handling this all by yourself."

"In the kitchen, having some breakfast."

Lucy nodded. "This is not an easy job." She turned to the little girl. "At least, you do not give us any trouble, do you, Jennie?"

The child removed her thumb from her mouth and rushed at Lucy. "Miss! Miss!" she cried, wrapping her tiny arms around Lucy's knees.

"Have a care, Jennie. You are liable to do Miss an injury." Lizzie threw up her hands as if to say it was all beyond her. "That's the most life I've seen in her for the past fortnight. Hasn't said two words all the time you was gone."

"*Were*, Lizzie." Lucy's correction was automatic. "All the time you *were*."

Lizzie shrugged. "What difference does it make how I talk? It won't change my life."

"You cannot know that If you watch the way you speak you can better yourself. Perhaps become a lady's maid, for instance."

"A clumsy thing like me? I can scarcely take care of children's clothes. Think on what I would do to all those lovely things what ladies wear. I would be put out the door before you could blink an eye."

Secure in her own skills, it had not occurred to Lucy that caring for a lady's toilette and accompanying wardrobe would be considered an impossible task. She stood corrected.

As if realizing his fit of rage was no longer the center of attention, William stopped screaming and got up from the floor.

"Miss?" he said. "Miss turn back?"

He toddled over to Lucy, his arms outstretched, waiting to be picked up. Before scooping him up, she disentangled herself from Jennie's embrace and with a parting kiss handed her over to Lizzie.

Setting up a rocking motion, which seemed to soothe the distraught William, Lucy addressed Lizzie. "I see he still does not pronounce his cees."

"I wouldn't worry about it, miss. It took my little brother Alfie, ever so long before he could talk proper."

Lucy ran a caressing hand over a large birthmark which disfigured the toddler's face. "William's fits of temper really concern me. I fear they do not bode well for his future."

Lizzie sputtered with mirth. "You have not had too much experience with kiddies, have you, miss? They are all little monsters at William's age. You shouldn't worry—he'll grow out of it."

Lucy was distracted from the conversation by a snuffling noise emanating from one of the cribs. She gave Lizzie a questioning look.

"That'll be Agnes. She was left on our doorstep. If the dogs hadn't kicked up a fuss over the comings and goings that night, the poor little thing would have most likely been dead by morning. By the look of her, she hadn't been fed properly since the day she was born."

Lizzie balanced Jennie on her hip and proceeded to rock the crib. "I tell you, miss, I don't know what the world is coming to."

Lucy peered into the crib. The baby's form barely showed under the blanket. She touched the tiny hand, which had escaped its swaddling, and it immediately clutched Lucy's thumb with a determination that surprised her.

"I think it would take a lot for this little one to give up on life," she said, her voice tinged with awe. "Have you ever seen such strength in one so small?"

"She's lucky someone brought her here. Sometimes the poor little babes would be better off if they just died, rather than face what fate has in store for them."

"Lizzie! It is sad to see such cynicism in one so young. How old are you?"

"Fourteen. You might call it cynicism—whatever that means—where I come from it's called facing facts."

Lucy shot her a look of sympathy. Her father, Josiah, had tried to protect her from the harsh realities of poverty, but she had seen and experienced enough to empathize with the other girl.

Nurse Wilcox returned from the kitchen, gave Lucy a brief nod, and addressed Lizzie. "Mrs. Young will be up soon, she is just finishing her breakfast."

"Mrs. Young?" Lucy asked.

"The new wet nurse. She was just about to wean her own babe when Agnes turned up on our doorstep last week."

It seemed to Lucy that there were times when life could be most providential. Without much more ado, among the three of them they fed and bathed the children, then took them outside for an airing. It was midafternoon before Lucy was able to tear herself away from them.

Their lessons completed, the older children were playing on the lawn. Most of them looked robust, their faces rosy with good health. A handful of newcomers, by contrast, looking pale and withdrawn, chose to stand on the sidelines and watch the activities of the others. At a signal from the teacher who was in charge, the children bobbed their heads to Lucy and chanted, "Good afternoon, Miss Garwood."

In return, she reined Daisy and said, "Good afternoon, boys and girls."

The formalities having been observed, the children returned to their play, and Lucy urged Daisy to a brisk trot. On her return to Northwycke Hall, she handed the mare over to a groom. To her surprise, Maude was sitting on the paddock fence, engaged in a conversation with Mickey. Maude waved to her and slipped off the fence, her face wreathed in a huge smile.

"Lucy, just the person I wanted to see." She turned to Mickey. "Good-bye, Mr. Dempsey, I enjoyed our conversation immensely."

Mickey touched his cap. "Only too 'appy to oblige, My Lady."

On leaving the stables, Maude linked arms with Lucy. Lucy gave her a quizzical look. "What on earth could you possibly find to discuss with Mickey? I thought you despised him."

Maude laughed. "A lady is allowed to change her mind. I find your Mr. Dempsey to be a fascinating fellow. He was explaining to me the finer points of picking pockets. Did you know that they sometimes work in teams?"

"No. The subject never arose."

"It seems that one person will create a diversion while another separates the lady or gentleman from their purse."

"It makes sense—by the way, Maude, there is a new baby at Hope House."

Maude gave Lucy's arm an impatient shake. "Please, Lucy, there is more. The pickpocket then passes the stolen item to another accomplice, who, in turn, passes it on to yet a third person. It seems it lessens the chances of being caught."

Lucy frowned. "Mickey had no business bringing up such a shameful subject. I must say I am disappointed in him and will not hesitate to tell him so."

Maude looked horrified. "Please, Lucy, do not utter a single word. It was I who brought up the subject."

Lucy looked askance. "Whatever for? All the years I have known Mickey I have never asked such a question of him. To be honest, I did not want to know. I have always had this dread of seeing him hanging from a gibbet, one day."

Maude squeezed her hand. "I am sorry, Lucy. It was very thoughtless of me. Look on the bright side—you will never have to worry about such a thing again. James is very pleased with the work he does with the horses."

Lucy allowed herself to be mollified. "Perhaps I worry too much. I suppose Harcourt has left for London?"

Maude sighed. "Yes, unfortunately. I expect now we have to await an invitation to visit the country seat of his parents. Harcourt—is that not a beautiful name?"

Lucy smiled. "I cannot say that I have given the matter too much thought. I must admit it seems awfully strange being on such familiar terms with the gentleman, but if he is going to be a member of the family…"

Maude sighed. "A member of the family. Does that not sound heavenly?"

Lucy laughed outright. "It is only natural for you to think so, Maude dear. You say you were looking for me? Was it to discuss this paragon you are going to marry?"

"Yes, it was, but please do not make fun of me, Lucy. I know I am being a trifle excessive, but in truth I do not seem to be able to help myself."

"Nor should you, Maude. I am sure that Harcourt Langley will make you an admirable husband, and I would be concerned for your happiness if you were not beside yourself with joy. Perhaps you should tell me what you want me for."

Maude colored. "I just wanted you to know that when I accepted his offer of marriage, he kissed me."

Lucy patted her shoulder. "How romantic. I am delighted for you."

"Romantic? It was the most terrifying moment of my life."

"Really? I find that most confusing."

"Do you not remember the reaction of a certain other gentleman upon kissing me? As far as His Grace was concerned it was not a memorable experience."

"But there was no love between you. Surely it was different when Harcourt kissed you."

A dreamy expression softened Maude's features. "Oh, yes. It was as you said it would be—which brings me to the reason I wanted to see you."

Lucy was mystified. "This gets more interesting by the minute. I fail to see how anything could possibly be the matter."

Maude clutched Lucy by the shoulders. "Do you not see? James is planning the wedding for next summer. To wait that long would be absolute *torture* for Harcourt and me."

Lucy thought of the kisses she had shared with Robert Renquist. "Oh dear me, yes. I see what you mean."

"It is no use, I must insist the date be moved forward."

Lucy gently disengaged herself from her grasp. "I do not think that is the way to go about it, Maude dear."

Maude looked stricken. "What do you suggest?"

"Your best strategy would be to have Emily intercede for you. She will remind James of the passion they share, and he will be helpless to resist."

"Really, Lucy?" She sounded hopeful, yet forlorn, rather like a small child who has begun to doubt the existence of

Father Christmas.

Maude has been denied very little in her life, Lucy thought. *Unlike the children of Hope House, who have known nothing but privation.*

Or unlike you, a small voice niggled away in her head. *Admit it, Lucy Garwood, you are awash in your own misery.*

Lucy brushed away such thoughts as unworthy. After all, thanks to the Northwycke Garwoods, her future looked far rosier than she had a right to expect. But if she could not spend the rest of her life with her one true love, it would be like attending a feast and being forced to eat sawdust.

Lucy lost patience with herself. It was not Maude's fault that fate had dealt her a kinder hand. "One cannot be sure, Maude," she replied, "but if anyone can convince James to let you marry sooner, it will be Emily."

Maude impulsively threw her arms around Lucy and kissed her on the cheek. "I do so hope you are right Next summer seems like an eternity."

"I quite agree," Lucy replied.

Maude smiled. "You are such an understanding soul."

Why would I not understand, Lucy thought. *Without Robert Renquist by my side, my life yawns before me like a book filled with blank pages.*

Fourteen

Robert sat in front of the library fire reading a copy of Lord Byron's "Childe Harold's Pilgrimage." In a fit of frustration he snapped the book of poetry closed and put it aside. Ever since the Garwoods had departed Linborough Castle, the simplest of pleasures no longer held his interest.

He got up and replenished the glass of brandy he had been sipping. Before he could return to his chair, the high-pitched voices of his sisters ripped the delicate fabric of peace within the castle walls. A laugh of glass-shattering intensity made him wince.

He put down his brandy and remained standing; knowing his sisters would soon bring their clamor into his sanctuary and assail his ears with the doings of their evening out Surely enough, within a few moments they breezed into the room, laughing ostensibly over a story they shared.

"From all the frivolity I would say you have had a very jolly evening."

Esther shook her blond curls, which were once more ringletted and beribboned, no doubt, he thought grimly, at Mother's behest. "Indeed we did, Robert, although I must admit your absence added a pall to the festivities. Viscount Rossmere lost considerable consequence by what could only be termed a snub on your part."

"Nonsense. I have not accepted any invitations for quite some time."

Esther pursed her lips. "It does not speak well of you, brother. As the ranking personage of the district, it is your social obligation to accept the invitations of the local gentry."

"Esther is right," Miriam chimed in. "And Mama is just as

bad. I am surprised at her for not going tonight She usually accepts the invitations of those she deems worthy of her gracious condescension."

"I say," Robert remonstrated. "Mother could hardly be expected to go with a sick headache."

"Hmmph!"

Robert could not decide whether this retort from Esther should be considered a snort or a sneer. Either way, he thought her attitude did nothing to enhance her charm.

"Mama has been enjoying these so-called sick headaches ever since you failed to follow through with your offer for Maude Garwood."

"Such a mean-spirited remark does you no credit Esther. Mother retired to her bed as soon as the both of you left for the Rossmeres."

Esther scowled. "In any case, she is wasting her time."

"What do you mean?"

"It was discussed over dinner this evening."

"For goodness sake, Esther, what are you talking about?"

"*I* will tell you," Miriam inteijected. "If it is left up to Esther we shall be up until cock crow."

Robert leaned his elbow on the mantel. "By all means exercise a little dispatch."

Miriam took a deep breath. "It is the latest *on dit*. It seems that Viscount Langley offered for Lady Maude."

"Is that all? I rather thought he would. I take it she accepted?"

"Oh, yes," Miriam replied, her eyes gleaming with excitement, "but the best part is they are to be married next Sunday by special license."

Esther gave a disdainful sniff. "Such haste is unseemly. It is a wonder the girl can hold up her head in polite society."

Robert laughed. "It is evident that you have never been in love, sister dear."

"And I suppose *you* have?"

"Perhaps."

"*Belle Amies*, do not count."

"What do you know of such things?"

135

"Good heavens, Robert Miriam and I are neither deaf nor blind. Mother has dragged us around to enough 'at homes' to afford us an endless supply of information on all manner of scandals and peccadilloes. I repeat *belle amies* and similar strumpets do not count."

Robert shrugged. "That narrows the field considerably." His mind dwelt on a pair of russet brown eyes and a full rosy mouth. The exercise filled him with longing. He laughed lightly. "It is probably safe to say that love has eluded me."

Esther put her hands on her hips. "I declare. I truly believe gentlemen are incapable of true love."

"You are probably right I have long suspected we do not merit the affection you fair ladies lavish upon us."

Esther gave him a penetrating stare. "For heaven's sake, Robert. You are completely and utterly foxed!" She cast her eyes down to Miriam's level. "I suggest we go to bed, sister. I refuse to encourage such foolishness."

She tilted her head at a haughty angle and departed the room. Miriam gave Robert a rueful shrug and trailed after her.

A few minutes later, Robert retired to his own chambers. His sleepy valet looked pleased to see him. Robert knew the hours he kept were hard on the manservant The smile on the man's face proved to be short-lived.

"I want to be packed and ready to go to the village of Northwycke by first light tomorrow." Robert paced back and forth as he barked out the order.

"Very good, Your Grace," the servant replied, his face not registering a flicker of emotion.

Robert wheeled round, almost knocking the slighter man off his feet "No. No. What am I thinking? The Garwoods will be busy with Lady Maude's wedding next weekend. The brandy must have addled my brain."

He became aware of a look of surprise on Sander's face. The brandy had also made him lose the impersonal air he normally adopted in the presence of servants. He resolved to drag himself up from the pit of self-indulgence into which he had descended in the weeks following his separation from

Lucy Garwood.

"We shall depart on Saturday. That should give me plenty of time to prepare for a visit to the Garwoods on the Tuesday or Wednesday."

The valet nodded. "Will that be all, Your Grace?"

"Yes, thank you. Get a good night's sleep, for a change. I doubt I shall be rising too early."

"Very good, Your Grace. I trust you will sleep well."

He bowed himself out of Robert's chambers with the deference usually reserved for royalty. When the door closed, Robert frowned. He sometimes suspected the man was mocking him. One never really knew what went on in the minds of the lower orders.

Baby Agnes was teething and had been crying fretfully all morning. Lucy walked the floor with her, very much aware that the ache she felt in her back was becoming increasingly more painful with each passing minute. She found it hard to believe that such a small bundle could prove to be such a burden. To make matters worse, Lucy suffered from an intense headache.

This she attributed to the harrowing nightmares that had disturbed her sleep the previous night She was no stranger to these dreams and they were always variations of the same theme. She would be pursued through the streets and alleyways of London by an angry horde armed with cudgels.

Miss Harris, her tormentor from the mantuamaker's, was invariably at the head of her pursuers, with cabbage soup still dripping from her hair and clothes, and screaming, "Don't let her get away. The wicked little besom deserves to hang!"

She hefted Agnes onto her other shoulder. Seemingly outraged by the change, the baby stiffened in her arms and howled even louder. Lucy thought her head would split in two.

Close to tears herself, Lucy moaned, "Please, oh please, little one, go to sleep, I beg of you."

"Here. Let me see to her, miss," said Lizzie, her face filled with concern. "You look proper worn out"

Lucy chose to ignore the remark. "You did not stay out very long." She gave Lizzie a questioning look. "What have you done with William and Jenny?"

"Nurse has them. Agnes here could be heard all over the place so she suggested I come and take over for you."

"That was kind of Mrs. Wilcox."

Lizzie laughed. "Kindness had nothing to do with it She was afraid you'd tire of the whole uproar and not come back. I don't know what we'd do without you."

"There is no fear of that. I came to Hope House with the intention of teaching the older children their lessons, but these little ones stole my heart."

"You'd best let me take Agnes before her bawling changes your mind for you."

Lucy handed the baby over to her. "Thank you, Lizzie. I think I will go down to the kitchen for a dish of tea."

Lizzie nodded. "Good idea. It will do you a world of good."

Upon seeing the younger girl coax a rag into Agnes's mouth, Lucy delayed her departure and watched with interest. At first the baby resisted, but soon she was sucking avidly, and as if by magic ceased to cry.

"Lizzie, what are you giving her?"

"Just a little brandy. She should be asleep in a minute or two."

Lucy was shocked. "Spirits? You gave that child spirits?"

"It wasn't very much and it took away her pain."

"But is it not harmful?"

Lizzie smiled. "Don't fret, miss. It was Dr. Mainwaring who left the brandy here for Agnes. We couldn't afford brandy, of course, but my mum used to rub dandelion wine on our gums when we was teething."

"I would never have dreamed of doing such a thing. I think I will go for that tea now."

"If you don't mind my saying so, miss, you look awful. You would be better off going right back to the Hall and straight to your bed. You'll be no use to anyone if you was to take sick."

Lucy smiled in spite of her headache. "You sound very

motherly. Tell me, Lizzie—were you ever a little girl?"

Lizzie shrugged. "My mum works in the dairy. There's five of us and I am the eldest"

"Could you be spared to work here?"

"The coppers I earn are needed at home. My sister, Elsie takes care of the others, now."

"Were you taught how to read or write?"

Lizzie looked mystified. "Good heavens, miss—what on earth for?"

What indeed? Lucy thought. She saw a life of drudgery and privation yawning ahead for Lizzie and all the other girls like her—especially if she were to marry and be saddled with more hungry mouths than she could afford to feed.

As if dismissing her lack of schooling as a subject not worthy of further consideration, Lizzie transferred her attention to Agnes. She gave Lucy a jubilant smile. "She's well away. Why don't you go home, miss? You'll feel a lot better in the morning."

"I do believe I shall. Thank you for your concern, Lizzie."

Deciding to forgo the tea, Lucy went to the stables and claimed Daisy. At first she allowed the mare to go at a brisk gallop, but finding it too jarring for her headache, she eased her into a gentle trot.

It was this series of events that put her at the top of the rise in time to see Robert enter the gates of Northwycke on his magnificent white horse, Sir Galahad.

On one level, she wanted to race Daisy across the meadow to intercept his path. How wonderful it would be to see his dear face once more! But reason prevailed. She was all too aware that marriage between them was out of the question.

The decision was taken out of her hands, for Robert chose that very moment to glance in her direction and reined his horse to a standstill and waited for her to catch up with him. The last few yards were the longest Lucy had ever ridden.

At her approach, Robert dismounted Sir Galahad and walked over to Daisy. He took Lucy completely by surprise by lifting her from her saddle and taking her in his arms.

He held her so close to his chest she thought she would

suffocate, and thought it did not matter. It was a small price to pay to be in his embrace, and with her last breath inhale his beloved scent. But this was not to be. Slowly he let her feet slide to the ground and with a groan, plundered her mouth with a kiss.

At first her lips parted to receive his, her ability to resist swept away by his ardor. Then to her dismay, her knees grew weak and her senses reeled. With a sharp cry, she pushed him away.

"For pity's sake, Your Grace, you shame me in full view of Northwycke Hall."

He released her and stepped back a pace. "Robert. Call me by my name, for heaven's sake. As to kissing you? God help me, Lucy, I could do no other. I have been longing to kiss you ever since that morning on the beach—have thought of nothing else, in fact."

"Miss Garwood. You must call me Miss Garwood." She put her hand to her mouth to cover a sob.

He pulled her to him and cradled her head on his shoulder. "My darling girl, do not cry. It is my wish to protect you from all that is unpleasant in this world, and to that end I am here to ask the marquess for permission to marry you."

Lucy pushed him away once more. "Dear heavens. Do not make this any more difficult than it is. I have told you that this cannot be—that my life must follow another path."

Robert grasped her by the shoulders. "Look me in the eye and tell me that you do not love me."

"I cannot do that You know that I love you—but that does not change anything."

Robot looked jubilant "Do not be so sure of that, darling girl. If you love me—anything and everything is possible. Did you not once tell me that your Cousin James would not make you marry where your heart does not lie?"

"Then you intend to pursue this matter?"

He kissed her lightly on the cheek. "I am duty bound. The Marquess of Northwycke is expecting me."

"Then I shall not keep you." She indicated a side path. "This is where we part company."

Robert gave her a questioning look.

"It is a shortcut to the stables."

"Allow me to help you remount"

"Thank you, no. I am in need of a walk."

After handing Daisy over to one of the stable boys, Lucy entered the Hall through the servants' entrance, taking care to go to her chamber via the back stairs.

She sat in a daze for several minutes and was about to get undressed when one of the chambermaids informed her that the master requested her presence in the library.

Lucy could see only one reason for this. James wished to know what she had done to encourage the Duke of Linborough's advances. It was with a high state of trepidation that she knocked on the library door.

"Please to enter."

James's tone was neutral, and she derived some comfort in that.

On her entry, he accorded her a quizzical stare. "Please be seated, Lucy."

She complied, sitting gingerly on the edge of the chair. It was one of a pair facing the hearth. To her dismay, James did not sit down but began to pace the floor. Lucy had lived under his roof long enough to know that this was a sign he was upset She gave him an apprehensive look.

"The Duke of Linborough just paid me a call."

"Yes, Cousin James, I know."

"Oh?"

"Our paths crossed when I returned Daisy to the stables. It seems to have been a very short visit."

"Yes, indeed. Have you any idea why he requested this audience?"

Ever honest, Lucy replied, "Yes, sir. He expressed a wish to marry me—but I told him it would be to no avail."

James stopped his pacing and gazed into the fire burning in the hearth. "I am sorry, Lucy, but you do understand that a marriage between you and Linborough is absolutely out of the question."

"Yes, Cousin James. I am not lacking in wits."

James turned to look at her. Lucy was aware that in her anguish she had overstepped her place.

"Please forgive my shortness. I realize it was untoward, but it could not have taken you more than a scant ten minutes to convince the gentleman as to the unsuitability of the match."

Try as she may, she could not keep the little catch out of her voice.

James placed a hand on her shoulder. "You must not blame His Grace. I made it very clear that I would not allow him to marry you. After that, the only thing left for him to do was to take his leave. One could hardly expect him to linger over brandy and small talk."

"I suppose not." Lucy was not deceived by James's version of what had transpired for a moment. She knew he was shouldering the blame for Robert's departure to spare her feelings, and she loved him for it.

"Absolutely. The gentleman has received a grievous blow to his pride. I doubt he will ever speak to me again. Perhaps you will tell me how this thing got started? The day you fell in the ocean, I suppose?"

Lucy shook her head. "It happened in the rose arbor in London."

James took a sharp intake of breath and chose that moment to sit in the chair opposite hers. He leaned forward. "Kindly explain."

Lucy obliged. Taking care not to miss a detail—even the part where the duke kissed Maude and realized his mistake. When she came to the conclusion of her little saga, James frowned.

"It seems that His Grace has been taking shocking liberties with the younger ladies of my household. I suppose I should call him out over the matter."

Lucy jumped out of her chair. "Oh, no. I beg of you, James. His Grace is a scholar—not a swordsman."

"If I thought otherwise, Lucy, I would not think twice of demanding satisfaction."

The wicked innuendo was lost on Lucy. "I assure you James.

I have seen nothing in the gentleman's deportment that would indicate a tendency toward the warlike arts."

"You really love him, do you not?"

"Alas, I truly do."

"That is the risk one takes when one treats the subject of kissing lightly. Remember, Lucy, there is no such thing as a harmless little kiss. Such a notion has been the undoing of many an innocent maid."

Lucy sighed. "Rest assured, James, I doubt I shall ever kiss another man as long as I live."

James rose. Lucy took this to mean that her interview was over. She stood also and dropped James a curtsy.

He responded with a slight bow, and added. "For one so young, Lucy, that is a very long time to go without a kiss. I suggest that in future you try to be a little more circumspect. At the very least, try not to kiss a gentleman who is in no position to offer you marriage."

Lucy felt her face flush a rosy red. She curtsied to James one more time, and fled the room.

Fifteen

Robert left Northwycke Hall full of mixed emotions. Anger and outrage predominated—mostly aimed at James Garwood, although the gentleman's mother came in for her share of his acrimony. What she had *not* said with regard to Lucy Garwood's lineage was every bit as suspect as that which she had implied.

He remembered all too well the slight smile and the almost imperceptible nod the dowager marchioness had accorded his mother on her assumption that Lucy came from the Shrewsbury branch of the Garwood family.

His hands tightened on Sir Galahad's reins. How dare James Garwood pass off the daughter of his father's by-blow as a distant cousin? Images of Lucy flitted through his mind. The emaciated fifteen-year-old avidly devouring the delicacies at Gunter's and then bravely facing him down when he had baited her. Her spirit was even more remarkable when one considered her background, and the ordeals she had faced. Such things would account for the certain earnest quality to her character.

He remembered seeing her kneeling in the garden at Mayfair, her face and clothes bedaubed in mud. Then, conversely, a more mature Lucy emerging from the ocean looking like a glorious sea-nymph. But it was the vision of Lucy standing in an arbor of white roses just before their very first kiss that tore him apart.

He grasped Sir Galahad's thick mane. "God help me," he groaned. "I still love her."

On returning to the Rose and Crown, he found Sanders buckling the straps to his luggage, a small trunk of finely tooled leather he had picked up in Florence in what seemed now to be a lifetime ago.

"Good, Sanders. Glad to see you are on top of things."

"We are returning to Linborough then, Your Grace?" The valet's voice was filled with hope.

"Not right away. Since we are so close to the City, I am desirous of going there first. Kindly see to it that Baines has the carriage ready for our departure as soon as possible. If we do not tarry, we should get to Mayfair in plenty of time for dinner."

"It is to be hoped they have suitable provisions to serve Your Grace an adequate meal."

"Good heavens, Sanders, I would not leave such a thing to chance. As soon as I decided to pay a visit to the house in Mayfair, I sent word to the London staff to expect me shortly thereafter. I find that a well-informed household is not so apt to burden one with unpleasant surprises."

Robert was shocked by his own loquacity. It was not like him to chatter away to servants. He supposed it was better than being left to his own thoughts. As far as he was concerned, this had to have been the worst day of his life.

After being away from Linborough Castle for several days, Robert found it soothing to bathe in the comfort of his own house. However, the meal the housekeeper provided for him, although well presented, did not pique his appetite. He attributed this to being overly tired. He found it somewhat disturbing when the next morning he derived no pleasure from his breakfast either.

Later in the morning, he drove his curricle to Piccadilly to visit Hatchard's, the booksellers. He was greeted most effusively by the proprietor, a slightly built man with a complexion the color of old parchment, for rather than avail himself of the library the establishment offered, Robert was known to buy any book that caught his fancy with little regard for the cost.

"I am so glad you paid us a visit, Your Grace, I have a book I think might interest you. It only came out this week, and is being well received by the more scholarly among the gentlemen."

"I see. Then I am safe in assuming that it is not a work of fiction?"

"Quite the contrary, Your Grace. It is written by the eminent scholar, Dr. Fielding."

"He finally finished his book on the world's philosophers, then?"

Mr. Hatchard's eyes widened. "You were privy to this knowledge, Your Grace? It came as a great surprise to the rest of us."

"I rather expect it did. And you are right I am most interested in acquiring a copy—two, in fact."

"*Two?*" He signaled to an assistant. "Two copies of *The World's Philosophers* for His Grace, if you please."

Robert knew by the eagerness expressed in the bookseller's voice that Fielding's work would cost him dearly. The shop assistant staggered to the counter, carrying the weighty tomes.

He opened one of them. "I see that Longman and Company published this. Send one of them to my house. I would be much obliged if it were to arrive before this evening. The other one I should like to go to a Miss Garwood, at Northwycke Hall. I assume you know its whereabouts?"

Mr. Hatchard nodded. "Lord Northwycke is gracious enough to patronize my establishment."

"Excellent I also expect you to have one of your staff deliver it to Northwycke, and for this I am willing to pay you well."

After refusing all offers of refreshments, Robert departed. He took over the curricle ribbons from Baines. Once the servant had assumed his position at the rear of the conveyance, the duke proceeded to the establishment of Longman and Company.

Within the hour, he had Dr. Fielding's address in his possession. He did consider waiting until the next day to pay his old teacher a visit, but decided to get the interview over with. The prospect of departing for Linborough Castle at first light was too tempting.

As the curricle made its way through Bloomsbury, he took note of the air of prosperity the tall, many-storied residences displayed. As he ventured further into the district, the houses began to take on an air of shabby gentility. Those of a decidedly seedy bent eventually replaced these.

If Lucy had not happened to mention that his erstwhile teacher lived in Bloomsbury, he would have thought the publisher had given him the wrong address. After a slight moment's hesitation, he knocked on the door.

A thin woman with wispy gray hair opened it. Robert was surprised by the stony-faced reception he received. It was as if well-dressed aristocrats knocked on her door every day of the week, and she was thoroughly bored with the whole idea. However, she *did* crane her neck to give the curricle a cursory glance before executing an indifferent shrug.

Upon hearing he was seeking Dr. Fielding, she indicated the stairs with a jerk of her head. "His rooms are on the left side of the landing." Without further ado, she disappeared down a long, dark passageway, leaving him to find his own way to Dr. Fielding's quarters.

When Dr. Fielding opened the door, Robert was surprised to see that the professor did not look as old as he had remembered. In fact, he perceived that the gentleman was quite handsome, probably no more than fifty years of age, and carried himself with a certain austere elegance. Robert concluded that with maturity, one regarded others in a different light.

He became aware that the scholar was subjecting him to equal scrutiny. "Are you not the Duke of Linborough's son? Came about that book I wrote, I suppose."

"In part."

"Please come in." He gestured toward a faded green armchair Robert suspected had not been in style since King George had incited the colonies to rebel. "Please be seated, my lord. I have a kettle boiling on the hob—perhaps I may offer you a dish of tea?"

"Thank you, no."

Dr. Fielding shrugged and sat down in the mate of the chair Robert occupied.

He steepled his fingers. "What may I do for you—Marquess of something or other, are you not? I had a difficult time keeping you all straight. There were so many of you over the years."

"I inherited my father's title about four years ago. I am sure it was tiresome trying to keep the offspring of the Philistines sorted out." Robert watched him closely to see if his remark would elicit a reaction from him. He was not disappointed.

Dr. Fielding's eyes widened a fraction. "That is one way of putting it, I suppose."

"It says it all, I would think."

He made a dismissive gesture. "You said my book was only part of the reason you are here. I am thinking the other part carries more significance."

"Although I took the liberty of purchasing two copies of your work, I must confess that you are correct in thinking so."

"Two copies? Most would balk at one. It makes for very dry reading for—"

"The average *Philistine?*"

"All the time I was at Oxford, not once did I give voice to such thoughts. No—not once. So how the devil…?" He snapped his fingers. "I have it You must know little Lucy Garwood—in fact know her very well, for such a subject to arise. Although for the life of me, I cannot imagine how your paths would cross—unless…" A thunderous expression crossed his face. "I suppose an innocent such as she would make easy prey."

Robert gave him a freezing stare, then realized his erstwhile tutor was not too far off the mark. After all, God help him, he had taken unpardonable liberties with Lucy's person, and then withdrawn his offer of marriage. Suddenly, he felt considerably less than noble.

He sought to allay his fears. "Rest assured, dear sir, Miss Garwood is safely in the care of her kinsman, the Marquess of Northwycke."

"James Garwood? Her mother, also?"

"Alas, no. I was given to understand the young lady is an orphan."

"I am grieved to hear that Harriet Garwood possessed all the womanly virtues." He remained silent for a while, as if reflecting on the aforementioned attributes of the deceased then punched one hand into the palm of the other. "I cannot for the life of me think how I failed to see the connection. Now come to think of it, her father, Josiah, bore a remarkable resemblance to the young sprout."

He fell silent for a moment, as if absorbing this new information, his eyebrows forming an unbroken ridge across his thin, aquiline nose.

"Of course, Josiah was in possession of a far more serious nature than the other one. He lacked his daughter's brilliance, but he soaked up everything I taught him like a sponge. Brothers, I suppose?"

Robert nodded. "I am curious, Professor. How did you become acquainted with the family? After all, I find it difficult to picture you frequenting the taverns of Limehouse."

"Good heavens, I should hope not. Josiah Garwood moved his family to Bloomsbury—at great personal sacrifice, let me add, when Lucy was nine. He had to work long hours to earn the few miserable coins extra it took to pay the rent here. They occupied the floor above this one."

"I see," Robert rejoined. This was part of the story James Garwood had omitted. Was it to deter him from the folly of an unsuitable marriage, or had her kinsman failed to question Lucy too closely?

"Do you?" Dr. Fielding sounded a trifle hostile.

"Hmm? Sorry, I did not hear the question."

"That is because none was posed. Forgive me if I appear to be blunt, Your Grace. At first, I thought you wished to discuss my book—a scholar's vanity—but it is patently clear you are here to inquire after the Garwoods. I suggest you get on with it."

"You are correct—although I must confess I was very elated when Miss Garwood told me of the great work you had undertaken. I hold you in great regard, Dr. Fielding, and wished to pursue our acquaintance further, but until I met Miss Garwood, I thought you had vanished off the face of the earth."

"That is most flattering. I am sure you are one of the few purchasers of my book who will actually take the trouble to *read* it. Most copies will simply gather dust on the shelves."

Robert agreed with his assessment, but rather than offer a false contradiction, he kept quiet. "Tell me, sir, what was it about this rag-and-bone man that caused you to form a friendship with his family? On the face of it, one would scarcely think you would find a common ground."

"I found him to be intriguing."

"Intriguing?"

"His was a fascinating story. Apart from that, how many rag-and-bone men of your acquaintance have the speech and deportment of a gentleman?"

Robert looked askance.

Dr. Fielding smiled. "Foolish question."

Robert nodded. "If Josiah Garwood was an educated person, why did he not aspire to a loftier position?"

"Your Grace, if a man were to apply to you for a position without a letter of recommendation would you hire him?"

"Perhaps not. But surely he could have gone to James Garwood once the latter assumed the title?"

Dr. Fielding shook his head. "You would have to be acquainted with Josiah Garwood to understand his nature. It was not in him to forward his own advantage at the expense of another. No. Even though James Garwood was a stranger to him, he would not have dreamed of adding to his distress by sullying the image of their father."

"Most commendable, I am sure, but such a waste of an education."

"His education was rudimentary, and if his fool of a father had not disowned him, I am sure he would have been an excellent pupil—more so than most of the paperskulls your class seems to turn out."

"Come now, Professor, that remark is a little extreme."

Dr. Fielding responded with a smile that Robert could only describe as mischievous. "Forgive me. But you must admit that for every lord in possession of your wit and intelligence, there are half a dozen like that bumbling old fool, Lord Crestwood."

Robert nodded in agreement.

"Of course," Dr. Fielding continued, "I have always held that the intelligence of the woman a man marries is far more important than her pedigree—that is, if he does not wish to raise a family of dullards."

"I doubt you would find many gentlemen willing to agree to

such an arrangement. Most of them could not think of anything worse than marrying a woman for her intellect"

"And I could not imagine anything worse than being saddled with a wife whose main concern in life is what sort of lace to sew on the bottom of her pantalettes." Dr. Fielding gave Robert a penetrating glance. "Neither can you, I am thinking."

Robert refrained from telling his erstwhile teacher that such undergarments were out of favor with the ladies—at least the ones he took to bed. In the meantime, he found the turn the conversation had taken to be too personal to suit his tastes.

Dr. Fielding looked speculative. "Could it be you harbor a *tendre* for Miss Garwood, and being of a prudent nature, wish to know more about her. No? I see by the expression on your face such is not the case."

Robert offered no explanation. He would prefer that the matter be dropped.

Dr. Fielding looked jubilant. "Of course! You have already approached the marquess on the matter and he was honor-bound to point out the unsuitability of the match. One can imagine the speed with which you departed that particular scene." He shot Robert a withering look. "Tell me, Your Grace, what did you hope to gain from this visit—confirmation that you did the right thing by deserting Lucy at the very first obstacle thrown in your path? Such devotion is touching."

Robert leapt to his feet. "See here, Fielding, you go too far."

Dr. Fielding rose also. "Do you think so, Your Grace? I think the opposite. I was under the impression that you intruded upon my privacy to get at the truth—and the truth is, Lucy Garwood is far too good for you." Indignation oozed from his every pore.

Robert stiffened. "I think I should leave. Thank you for your time, Dr. Fielding."

"Before you go, Your Grace. Consider this. If a gang of pickpockets had raised you, what do you suppose you would have grown up to be?—that is, assuming you would have survived to adulthood? Josiah Garwood not only overcame his past, he worked long hours at an onerous but honest occupation to take care of his family the best way he knew how. Lucy Garwood is a daughter anyone could be proud to claim as their own."

"Dr. Fielding, you will get no argument from me. I have been a bachelor far longer than most in my position." Robert paused to smile. "It took me a while to realize it, but I too have no desire to marry a young lady who is overly preoccupied with how much lace to sew onto her pantalettes."

Dr. Fielding's expression softened. "I meant every word I said, but perhaps my regard for the Garwoods has made me too harsh in my defense of them. I was certainly disrespectful of your rank. For this, I apologize."

Robert placed a placating hand on his shoulder. "Would that I had such a loyal friend. I should like you to hear my side of the story. You see, the Marquess of Northwycke presented Miss Garwood's situation in the worst possible light—seemingly in an effort to shock me into retracting my offer."

"I am sure he was trying to make it easy for you to get out of an embarrassing situation," Dr. Fielding inserted. "After all, most gentlemen would not countenance such a marriage. What on earth was he about—introducing Lucy to a situation that could only result in heartbreak for her?"

Robert felt a little sheepish. "It did not occur to him that I would fall in love with her—you see, I was courting his sister, Lady Maude. I did not offer for Lucy until his sister was safely married to Viscount Langley."

"Most circumspect of you."

"I am sure that with a suitable dowry, he folly intends to marry Lucy to a respectable country squire." Dr. Fielding looked shocked. "That brilliant young mind, married to some clod vegetating in the shires? I can think of nothing worse. It will not do. No. Not at all. Surely Northwycke can see that?"

"Set your mind at rest, sir. From the start, the marquess assured Lucy she had the freedom to choose her own path."

These words seemed to have a calming effect on Dr. Fielding. Then he sighed. "As far as I can see, there is no place within the structure of our society for females of intelligence. They are ridiculed, reviled—certainly not sought after as wives.

Small wonder some of them react by aping men—indulging in all manner of scandalous behavior."

It was Robert's turn to come to Lucy's defense. "You should not mention such creatures in the same breath as you speak of Miss Garwood. She is a virtuous young lady, and possesses too much common sense to embark on such a self-destructive path."

"Bravo. Have I not been saying so all along? I was merely expressing a hope that she is able to live a rich, fulfilling life." He held out his hand "Think long and hard, Your Grace. True love is a rare commodity."

Robert accepted Dr. Fielding's hand and shook it. "I want to thank you for your words of wisdom. I cannot say that they were easy to take but I know they were uttered in sincerity."

His old teacher smiled. "Listening to advice is a lot like having foul-tasting medicine thrust down one's throat. It is most unpleasant but might improve one's condition."

Robert had much to ponder as he departed Bloomsbury. His reaction to the confrontation with Dr. Fielding had been completely out of character. He had not only allowed a man of lesser rank to take appalling liberties, but had actually engaged in a dialogue with him which had revolved around the most private aspects of his life.

It was plain to Robert that the very fabric of his character was unraveling. What was happening to the aloof pride that had always served him so well when dealing with others? Even as a child, he had eschewed close friendships with other boys. In a flash it occurred to him that his mother was responsible for his standoffish ways. Had she not always impressed upon him the importance of keeping one's distance—lest other boys take advantage of one to further their own selfish interests?

Robert smiled to himself. What would Mother say if he were to inform her that not only had she entertained the daughter of a rag-and-bone man, but she would also have to accept her as a member of the family? He found the thought so delicious, he laughed out loud.

He reined in the pair of matched blacks pulling the curricle. He had just been indulging in idle fancy—but was marrying

Lucy such a bad idea?

Of course, he would not dream of exposing her past to anyone—much less his mother. In spite of her urgings for him to marry, he had an idea she would do her best to make the life of any girl who usurped her position as Duchess of Linborough an unmitigated hell.

"Thank heavens for Dower Houses!" he exclaimed.

Baines leaned forward. "Beg pardon, Your Grace?"

Without turning, Robert waved him off. "'Twas nothing, Baines. I was just remarking on how dark the sky is turning. It is to be hoped we make it back to the house before the rain starts."

"Please don't spare the horses on my account, Your Grace. I can hang on."

"I rather thought you would say that" Robert gave the ribbons a snap, and the horses set off once more, but at a far brisker pace.

Lucy placed her hand on eight-year-old Mary Simpson's forehead. It was hot to the touch. She nodded to the young teacher who had brought the child to her. "I am afraid your suspicions are correct, Miss Smith. She has come down with the grippe. Do you not think at this point we should turn the girl's dormitory into a sickroom and let the girls who have yet to come down with it sleep in the infirmary?

The mousy Miss Smith looked doubtful. "Better consult with Nurse Wilcox, she's very jealous of her position."

"I am afraid Nurse Wilcox has taken to her own bed with the grippe, and is, no doubt, past caring as to who holds the reins of authority." Lucy rolled up her sleeves. "The sooner we get the dormitory ready for the sick children, the better."

"We?" Miss Smith wrinkled her nose. "Surely you do not expect me to demean myself in such a manner?"

Lucy gave her a look. Miss Smith bridled. "I have to return to my classroom. Heaven knows what those horrid little creatures are about."

Lucy pulled the little girl closer to her. "Tell me, Miss Smith, if you feel that way about children, why did you become a teacher?"

Miss Smith sniffed. "I only intend to stay long enough to get a letter of recommendation, then I shall seek a position teaching children more worthy of my attention."

Lucy raised a brow. "Really, Miss Smith? I doubt such children exist."

Miss Smith gave her hair a smug pat. "It is very gratifying to be appreciated by a young lady of quality."

"Oh?" Lucy arched her brow. "And who might she be?"

The woman looked confused.

"Take care not to take ill, Miss Smith, for I doubt there is anyone at Hope House worthy enough to take care of you."

Miss Smith bridled. "I have never been so insulted."

Lucy smiled sweetly. "My apologies, perhaps I misunderstood. I thought you were saying the people of Hope House were beneath you."

Miss Smith turned red, and flounced out of the infirmary. "Good riddance," Lucy muttered. "As soon as this sickness has run its course, I am going to have a talk with James about her. I would not have such as she in charge of the dog kennels, much less a schoolroom."

Lucy handed the little girl over to one of the scullery maids who had been pressed into service in the sickroom. "Another one for you, Millie. Dr. Mainwaring should be here shortly."

"I hope so, miss." She hesitated. "I am glad you put that haughty little madam in her place. If you ask me, She has a very high opinion of herself."

Not wanting to snub the girl, Lucy responded with a faint smile. She realized she had overstepped the mark in bringing the schoolmistress to task in front of a servant, but she could not be induced to feel remorse. Besides, there were far more important issues demanding her attention.

Before consulting with the housekeeper about clean linens for the girl's dormitory, Lucy stopped by the nursery. Jenny sat on the floor, playing with a wooden doll one of the carpenters at the Hall had fashioned. Lizzie sat rocking William's cot by pulling a rope attached to her foot. This freed her to hold Agnes in her lap.

Lucy looked at William. He lay quietly on his side, his face flushed with fever. "How long has he been this way?"

"I don't know, miss. He was fine when I put him down last night I don't like it—it's not like him to be so quiet."

"Wash him down with a cold cloth, and see if you can get him to take some of the barley water."

"I suppose he should go to the infirmary."

"No!"

Lizzie flinched.

Lucy swept her hand across her forehead. "I am sorry, Lizzie. I did not mean to shout at you—only I have not the heart to move a sick little boy from familiar surroundings. He would be terrified."

"Won't he give it to the other two?"

Lucy shook her head. "It is too late to worry about it They have been exposed."

"Oh dear."

"Not everyone catches the grippe, Lizzie. The most unlikely people are spared."

"Even so, Nurse Wilcox will have a thing or two to say about the matter," Lizzie opined. "I like her, and all that, but she is very—you know…"

Lucy smiled. "Yes, I know, but you should not talk about Nurse in that manner. She takes her responsibilities very seriously. That is not entirely a bad thing."

Lizzie made a moue. "You would find something good to say about the devil himself, miss."

"At the moment, Nurse is too sick to care what we do," Lucy said.

"What a shame." She had a wide grin on her face.

Lucy did not have the heart to chastise her. Heaven knows, there had been precious little to laugh about in the past few days.

On her arrival at Hope House three days prior, the symptoms of the grippe had shown up in four of the children. She had sent to Northwycke Hall for some of her clothes and had stayed at the children's home ever since. She did not want to run the risk of carrying the infection to Northwycke lest the sickness be passed on to James Elias. Little ones did not always survive the illness. It was also likely that some of the staff at the children's home would contract the disease, and therefore her help would be needed even more than usual.

She stroked William's cheek, then with great reluctance went to consult with Miss Davies, the housekeeper. Miss Davies was a small, prim little spinster with the lively, birdlike qualities characteristic of some Welsh women.

Together, they had fresh linens on the beds in the girls' dormitory by early afternoon. Soon they were occupied by patients of both sexes, twenty-seven in all; girls on one side, boys on the other.

For the sake of propriety, the straitlaced Miss Davies insisted on separating the sexes by erecting a screen down the center of the room, consisting of sheets, tablecloths, and even a newly laundered horse blanket borrowed from the stables. Personally, Lucy was of the opinion that their young patients were too ill to care one way or another.

"One must protect the innocence of these poor little lambs," Miss Davies said in a lyrical Welsh accent.

Once the infirmary was emptied of patients, Miss Davies sniffed the air and wrinkled her nose. "Indeed to goodness, this place could do with a good cleaning."

They commandeered buckets and hot water from the kitchen and with each of them armed with a scrubbing brush and a large bar of green soap got on their hands and knees and began to scrub.

It did not take long for Lucy to feel the bite of the strong soap. By the time the chore was two-thirds completed, her hands were red and almost to the point of bleeding. At the sound of footsteps crossing the planked floor, she stopped her scrubbing and was about to arch her back when a pair of men's top boots stopped directly in front of her.

They were black, and highly polished, with turnover tops of a rich shade of brown. Only a gentleman of substance could afford such fine boots. Her eyes traveled upward until she found herself staring into a pair of deep blue eyes. From their expression, Lucy assumed that the Duke of Linborough was not well pleased with what he saw.

"What the devil do you think you are doing?"

Lucy felt her hackles rise. "I believe it is called scrubbing, Your Grace."

"Please do not spar with me. I am well acquainted with the notion. I am merely inquiring as to why you see fit to take it upon yourself to perform such a menial task."

He seized her by the elbows and hauled her to her feet, then held her hands to scrutiny. "For pity's sake, your fingers are rubbed raw. Why did you not leave this job to someone more seasoned?"

Without waiting for a reply, he pulled her toward the door. "Do me the kindness of coming outside; we have to talk."

Miss Davies waved her on. "Do as the gentleman asks. One of the others can finish up."

Once outside, Lucy took a deep breath. It felt good to get away from all the sickness. Robert did not stop walking until they were hidden from sight by a planting of shrubbery.

He tried to embrace her, but she pushed him away.

"Kindly state your business, Your Grace, then let me get on with mine. There are a lot of sick children to care for."

His arms dropped to his sides. "I am well aware of the illness raging through this place. You should not risk your life for these urchins."

Lucy recoiled. "I wonder if you would be of the same opinion if they were *your* brothers or sisters?"

"I am not denigrating the importance of the children. I cannot help it if I place a higher value on your safety, or that of my family. It is only natural, and you know it."

"Do I? Such arrogance. What makes you think the lives of Renquists or Garwoods are any more precious than those of these little ones? If you prick them, do they not bleed?"

Robert threw up his hands. "Good heavens, Lucy. I came to propose to you—not to listen to you chastise me with a garbled version of Shakespeare. I swear, you are the only girl in all of England who would do such a thing."

"Then more's the pity. I—er—what did you just say?"

He kissed the palms of her hands. "You will be lucky if they do not blister. I said that I have come to ask you to do me the honor of becoming my bride."

Lucy's eyes widened. "Does James know of this?"

"Of course. I told him I was willing to overlook your unfortunate parentage."

Lucy clenched her hands, fighting off the urge to slap him. "How kind of you, Your Grace. I am *overwhelmed* by your gracious condescension."

He gave her a sharp look. "Do not tease, Lucy. I have been through too much this past few days. I was going to suggest we wait until you turned seventeen before we married—but have changed my mind. I want to marry you right away before any more obstacles are thrown in our path, then I suggest we spend our honeymoon on the Continent—somewhere warm—what do you think?"

"You may go to the devil as far as I am concerned."

"Good! I thought you would—did I hear you aright?"

"Oh, I think so, Your Grace. I happen to have had the best parents in the world. I fear the same may not be said of you— otherwise, you would know better than to call a lady's upbringing in question in the very same breath you ask for her hand."

"I apologize. Perhaps I did not choose my words wisely." He grasped her hand. "Try to see it from my viewpoint The details your uncle divulged about your background—and believe me, even the fact that a distant cousin turned out to be your uncle was shock enough—it was a lot to absorb all at once." He pulled close. "Please let us not quarrel—say you will marry me."

She pulled away from him. "Robert, I have no wish to quarrel with you, but I cannot marry you. We would both be miserable. You are far too proud to come to terms with who I am, and I am not about to grovel at your feet in eternal gratitude because you deigned to marry me."

"You seem to have a very low opinion of me," he said stiffly.

Lucy sighed. "Not at all. You cannot help being that you are, any more than I can. Do you not see? There is too wide a gulf between us."

"There is nothing I can say that can induce you to change your mind?"

Lucy shook her head. She could feel a tear roll down her cheek.

Robert wiped it away with his thumb. "You are quite unlike any other girl I have ever met. I think, perhaps, that high intelligence in a woman may be more of a curse than a blessing." He bent down and kissed her cheek. "Good-bye then, my little sea nymph. Alas, it is not in me to beg."

Lucy watched him stride away until he veered toward the stables and was no longer in sight. She fought the urge to follow, knowing in all probability she would never see him again.

A robin trilled in the hedgerow as if it were just another ordinary day. Lucy knew that for her ordinary days were a thing of the past. The sun could not shine bright enough, nor the birds sing sweet enough, to lighten the sorrow she carried in her heart.

Sixteen

By the end of the following week, the grippe had run its course, but not before claiming Lucy as its final victim. There were no fatalities; this, Dr. Mainwaring attributed to the grace of God, as two of the older people in the village had died.

As soon as Lucy was well enough, Maude's mother insisted she be moved to the Dower House. To Lucy's surprise, the dowager marchioness fussed over her like a mother hen, even to the point of spoon-feeding her broths and soups.

Lucy found this hard to understand, for whereas the lady had graciously allowed her to remain at Northwycke Hall, she had hitherto maintained a certain air of aloofness between them. Now she sat working on her embroidery in Lucy's room and anticipated her every need.

When Lucy was well enough to come down and join her for dinner, she positively beamed. "You have made an excellent recovery, Lucy dear. I should imagine that in a month or so you will be able to accompany me for a nice visit to Bath. The waters will do you an inordinate amount of good, and we can attend so many functions. You see—it will be most enjoyable."

It occurred to Lucy that she had been pressed into taking Maude's place. While very flattering, it was also something of a shock. Without having a say in the matter, decisions were being made for her future with alarming rapidity. Even so, she sympathized with the older woman.

"You must miss Maude very much," she said softly. The dowager's eyes misted. "Yes. I do. I tried to tell her not to be in such a hurry to marry young Langley—oh, he is nice enough, I suppose." She leaned over and whispered conspiratorially, "Even the best of gentlemen commit unspeakable acts upon

161

the persons of their wives. It is very hard to see one's little girl married, knowing she will have to suffer such indignities."

She patted Lucy's hand. "But of course, you must have realized this—why else would you have refused the Duke of Linborough's offer? I must say I was surprised. After that shameful business of falling in the ocean, and letting him see you soaking wet, I was sure you were trying to trick him into marriage."

"Lady Northwycke!" Lucy exclaimed. "It was an accident. At the time I was not even aware of His Grace's presence on the beach."

"I know that now. It was fortunate he happened along. He saved your life."

Lucy nodded in agreement, relieved she had not delved any deeper into her reasons for not having accepted Robert Renquist's offer. She wondered now if the early stages of the grippe had not addled her brains. The pride, which had inspired the rejection of his proposal of marriage, paled in importance against the longing she now felt to be in his arms once more.

"Of course, in my opinion, you should have accepted his offer. I know of no other young lady in your position—or even one well-dowered, for that matter, who would have refused him." She gave Lucy a probing look. "Was the idea of marrying him *so* distasteful?"

"No, madam. I happen to love him."

Lady Northwycke placed her fork on her plate. "Then what reason could you possibly have had, for refusing him?"

"Pride. He belittled my family."

"Good heavens, girl. Have you any idea how difficult the thought of marrying beneath his station must have been for him? From the moment he was old enough to understand such things, he has been made aware of his rank. Dukes can be every bit as top-lofty as princes of the blood-royal."

Lucy nodded. "Rag-and-bone men instill the same foolish pride in their daughters, it would seem."

Lady Northwycke raised her eyes to the ceiling. "What an odd girl you are. You profess to love the man, and yet spurned his offer. Most girls would have married him even if he were in possession of two heads, and had not one good thing to say about their families with either one." She shrugged. "In any case, the whole subject is now academic."

"Oh?" A death knell tolled in Lucy's head.

"Of course, having been indisposed, you would not have heard."

It took all of Lucy's fortitude to respond. "Heard what, madam?"

"The Duke of Linborough is now escorting Lady Caroline Barclay all over London."

"L-lady Caroline Barclay?" Lucy echoed, her voice barely above a whisper.

"Yes. It surprised me too—until I was told her pimples have cleared up quite nicely." She patted Lucy's hand. "Never mind, dear. No gentleman is worth the loss of a good night's sleep. This winter you shall accompany me to Italy, and will forget all about His Grace in no time at all."

She did not respond to Lady Northwycke's remark. Lucy was certain if she lived to be a hundred she would die with Robert Renquist's name on her lips.

As the days went by, Lady Northwycke quickly wove Lucy into the warp and weft of her own life. It was not long before she was accompanying the dowager on her charitable rounds among the cottagers.

Lucy liked talking to the country people. She especially enjoyed the way the old widows assumed that Lady Northwycke was an integral part of their lives. It was plain to see that most of them adored her.

She admired the dexterity the dowager displayed in handling the gig she used for her errands. She would urge the horse through the village lanes, visiting one house after another with the assurance of a messenger of God.

On departing the cottage of one toothless old dear, Lucy could not help but remark on the kindness she had shown the old woman. "It is so thoughtful of you to take her special broths and aspics, she must have great difficulty chewing solid foods."

Lady Northwycke looked surprised. "Why would I not do so? It is my duty to see to the welfare of our people."

"I am beginning to understand that, madam." She attempted to help the dowager into the gig, but was waived off. "I had no idea ladies of quality spent so much time caring for their people."

Lady Northwycke laughed. She took the reins of the horse, then turned to Lucy. "Good heavens, child, what did you think we do all day—sit on cushions of satin, eating strawberries and clotted cream?"

Lucy looked sheepish. "As a matter of fact, yes—wearing your diamond tiaras, of course."

Lady Northwycke wagged a finger at her. "I do not believe you think that for a moment, you dreadful girl."

"Perhaps I exaggerate, but only slightly."

The dowager gave her an indulgent smile. "I must confess that I have admired the work you have done at Hope House. Not many young girls would give so much of themselves. I am even told that you are not above the most menial of tasks."

Lucy grasped at the opportunity to regain her old life. "How gracious of you to say so, madam." She took a deep breath. "Now that I have recovered my strength, I feel I should go back. My help is sorely needed."

"Nonsense. I think it is perfectly proper for you to visit with the little ones, but my son does not wish you to work there anymore—in fact, he absolutely forbids it. You almost worked yourself into an early grave. At one point, we thought we were going to lose you."

"But the little ones need the attention."

"And to that end, James has hired another nursery maid."

"But—"

"Not another word. By the way, James also took care of that matter of Miss Smith, the schoolmistress you disliked. You might be pleased to hear she has been replaced by a young woman who displays a kinder attitude towards those less fortunate than herself."

"It was very good of Cousin James."

Lady Northwycke's expression softened. "My son is a very good man—but of course, you know that."

"Yes, I do. Most gentlemen do not have such generous hearts." She touched Lady Northwycke's sleeve. "You must take credit for the goodness that both your children display. You are all so kind and caring." As Lucy spoke, she contemplated the full extent of the generous spirit displayed by all of the Northwycke Garwoods.

"You are a good girl, Lucy, and that is thanks enough. By the way, I have advised James to hire an abigail for you."

"But—"

She raised an admonishing hand. "Now, Lucy, no more 'buts,' if you please. I know the idea of an abigail is distasteful to you, but it cannot be helped. It is impossible to participate in the social round without one of the creatures."

Lucy bowed to the inevitable. A lady who had been bathed and clothed by others all her life would not understand the modesty of one unused to such practices. She could not foresee ever being comfortable about it.

Actually, it took less than a fortnight for Lucy to get used to attentions of an abigail. Beth Hoxie, the servant in question, was a pert-faced woman of indeterminate years with an abundance of dark brown hair, which she wore in a bun on top of her head, and an outrageous sense of humor.

On learning of Lucy's inexperience with personal servants, and the undue modesty that went with this lack, the abigail affected an air of great seriousness.

"You have me worried, Miss Garwood. Is there something I should be told? Some terrible secret you have yet to divulge?"

Lucy felt confused. "What do you mean?"

"I once had a mistress who had three breasts. Mind you, the third one was small enough to be of no significance—tucked snugly beneath her left one. All the same, I almost swallowed my tongue when I first helped her with her bath." She gave Lucy a sly smile.

"You would not be planning to shock me with some-such, now would you, miss? Once is enough for anyone's constitution."

Lucy was about to offer an earnest denial when she caught a twinkle in her eye and laughed instead. "I fear, Miss Hoxie, I am going to have great difficulty in believing a word you say."

"I think not," she said with a chuckle. "You saw through me right away—and by the way, call me Hoxie."

"Not even Beth?"

She shook her head. "Just Hoxie, plain and simple. I have not been called Beth in so long I am apt not to answer to it."

"Very well. Hoxie, it is."

Lady Northwycke intended to spend a month in Bath, and jealous of her privacy arranged to rent one of the elegant houses on the Royal Crescent. The owner was out of the country, seeing to his estate in Jamaica, and was pleased to let it to a member of the *ton*. It was not fully staffed, but sufficient to cater to the needs of two ladies and their servants.

Lucy had scarcely been in the city of Bath for a week when she admitted to herself to not only having adjusted to the idea of having a body servant, but to reveling in it. The social scene was such it seemed she did nothing but change her clothes all day long. Lady Northwycke had spoken the truth. Without an abigail, it would be impossible.

The lady had been right on another point. Attending the baths *did* improve Lucy's sense of well-being. She did not know whether to attribute her growing strength to the warmth of the baths, or the extreme thirst generated by being immersed in them, which was later slaked, by taking the waters in the Pump Room.

The Pump Room was a favorite haunt of Lady Northwycke's. She loved to take Lucy's arm, visiting with this one and that. "No, you are not mistaken, Lady So-and-So," she would say, "my daughter, Lady Maude, did indeed, marry the Viscount Langley. Allow me to present Miss Garwood, a distant cousin." Then she would add, "You are quite right, of course, Lady So-and-So. She does bear a remarkable resemblance to my daughter." Being a titled lady of great consequence, she did not lack for company, and repeated this story to a fare-thee-well.

They were also invited to the theater as guests of the

Fotheringhams, for a revival of Oliver Goldsmith's comedy, *She Stoops to Conquer*. It was Lucy's first theater-going experience, and she was absolutely enthralled.

On hearing this, Lady Northwycke said, "I suppose it would be. We were far too busy with Maude's come-out. No matter. Next Season, we shall not only indulge in theater-going, we shall also attend the opera. You would like that, would you not?"

"Oh, yes, madam," Lucy responded fervently, "very much so."

Lady Northwycke gave her a wry look. "I should imagine you will be one of the few young ladies in attendance who will pay attention as to what is taking place on the stage. For the most part, the rest of them will be far more concerned with their own personal attire."

"I fear it is their own loss, my lady. How can they *not* be moved by such beauty and splendor?"

The dowager smiled. "Then you will not be too upset to hear that tomorrow night we shall be attending a concert featuring the music of the late Mr. Mozart?"

On hearing this piece of news, she could not believe her good fortune. It did not lessen her grief over losing Robert, but she had been taught at a very early age that one had to deal with whatever came along in life.

"People like us cannot afford to dwell on our misfortunes," her father had said. "Otherwise we would not survive." Lucy had too great a curiosity for life to stop living, and tomorrow, she told herself, she would hear the music of Mozart for the very first time.

The next evening, Lucy sat in openmouthed wonder as she listened to the orchestra bring the composer's music to life. On the ride home she did not utter a word until their carriage turned the corner to Royal Crescent, then she said, "The Season is such a long way off."

"Hmm?" Lady Northwycke replied. "Of what possible interest could the Season be to you, dear? After that debacle with the Duke of Linborough, you will not be going to private parties, or receiving others."

"Nor should I want to, madam. But after attending the concert this evening, waiting to experience the opera is going to be sheer torture for me."

Lady Northwycke patted her hand. "Nonsense. It will give you something to look forward to."

Those members of the *ton*, who happened to espy the Duke of Linborough and Lady Caroline riding their horses along Rotten Row in Hyde Park agreed they made a very handsome couple. As far as Robert was concerned, Lady Caroline was a vapid creature, but he grudgingly allowed that she rode well.

He tried to engage her in conversation, but when the topic showed signs of veering toward the cerebral, she gave his shoulder a playful tap with her riding crop, and with a flutter of her eyelashes, declared, "La, Your Grace, surely you do not mistake me for a bluestocking? Such creatures have my undying pity."

He inclined his head, "My apologies, Lady Caroline. I am certain a young lady as beautiful as you is much more at ease discussing—Hmm, let me see…" He gave her a sly grin. "Lace?"

"Lace, Your Grace?"

"Lace. Alencon, Mechlin—"

"*Lace*—but of *course!* Lace."

She spent the next fifteen minutes singing a paean to the virtues of lace. By the time she was through, his head was spinning and he knew more about lace and its applications than he cared to think about. "Were they still in favor, she would be in possession of die fanciest pantalettes in all of England," he muttered under his breath.

She leaned toward him. "Forgive me, Your Grace, but I did not quite catch what you were saying."

He gave her a beatific smile. "My dear Lady Caroline, I was merely admiring the feathers on your hat. You cut a very dashing figure."

When he returned her to the bosom of her family, he said, "Do not forget the musicale my mother is hosting tomorrow evening. I do believe your family agreed to attend."

"Oh yes," she replied, batting her beautiful blue eyes at him. "I would not miss it for the world."

Robert saw a glimmer of hope for them, but her next remark took care of that.

"I have the most beautiful new dress. It is positively *dripping* with lace and I am just *dying* to show it off."

On the way home, it was Sir Galahad who set the pace. Robert was too preoccupied with his own thoughts to even notice. On passing Mayfair Court, he gave Northwycke House a cursory glance. He knew the Garwoods were not in residence.

He wondered if Lucy was still playing the drudge at the orphan asylum, and he smiled wryly. Of all the girls in the world, why had he fallen in love with such an oddity? How much simpler life would be if he could bring himself to marry a beautiful goose-brain—Lady Caroline, for instance?

After leaving Sir Galahad with a groom, he entered the house, taking care to walk lightly—he was in no mood to engage his mother in conversation. Unfortunately, she was coming out of her sewing room at precisely the same moment he was handing his hat and riding crop to the butler.

On seeing him, her face lit up. "Robert, darling, just the person I wanted to see. Do come in and share a coze."

He bowed to the inevitable. "Very well, Mother." He turned to the butler. "Palmer, a large brandy if you please." He inclined his head in his mother's direction. "Would you care for anything?"

"A small sherry, I should think."

As soon as Palmer withdrew from the room, Robert took a sip of brandy, then opened the conversation. "Tell me, Mother, which direction do you wish this coze to take? Shall we be discussing the latest fashions, or the declining power of the East India Company?"

She gave him a freezing look. "What is it this time, Robert? Is the girl lacking in conversation—or does she talk too much?" She gestured with her index finger. "Wait—could it be that Lady Caroline is too beautiful, or has the girl who would suit your peculiar tastes yet to be born? Tell me, son. I really would like to know."

This time, Robert gulped his brandy. His mother was in fine form. "If you must know, parrots conduct more intelligent conversations than the young lady in question."

"Is that all? If you wish for intelligent conversation, go to your clubs. A girl does not produce an heir with her wits. Neither does a man. If such were the case, you never would have been born."

"Mother!"

She shrugged. "Well, it is true. You inherited your brains from my side of the family. I could have married one of the most brilliant scholars of our time, but when your father offered for me, I considered it my duty to accept."

"Your duty?"

"A curate's stipend scarcely kept the roof over our heads. My poor papa had to work a farm to put food on the table and clothes on our backs." She sipped her wine. "When your father offered for me, how could I turn my back on my family by refusing? Also, was it not my duty to my unborn children to ensure they did not grow up under similar circumstances?"

"I see." It occurred to Robert that this hitherto unmentioned addition to his mother's list of sacrifices was perhaps her greatest claim to martyrdom. "It could not have been easy for you."

She gave him a defiant look. "I have never regretted the choice I made. Granted, your father and I were not a love match, at least not on my part, but we rubbed well together, and you children benefited because of it."

"I derive no pleasure in knowing that my place in society was secured at the expense of my mother's happiness."

She smiled wistfully. "There is a certain satisfaction in knowing that one has done one's duty by one's family— besides, to be perfectly honest, I rather *like* being the Duchess of Linborough."

Robert burst out laughing. "Mother, I love you. There is not another person in the whole wide world quite like you."

She looked surprised. "I fail to see the humor in this.

Marriage is a very serious matter."

He leaned over and kissed her cheek. "I quite agree, darling, but we do not share the same views on the subject. It is hard to believe we share the same blood."

"Your father can be blamed for your strange ideas. It would have served you better had you inherited my practical ways. You would have presented the Linboroughs with an heir long ago."

"I suppose there is something to what you say. Tell me, Mother, who was this scholar whose heart you broke?"

"Do you really wish to know?"

"I would not ask if it were otherwise."

"It was your precious Dr. Fielding."

Robert's eyebrows almost disappeared into his hairline. "Where on earth did you meet him?"

"In church. We grew up in the same parish."

"The devil, you say." Robert gave her a speculative look. "Of course, Mother, you realize you have just exposed your darkest secret."

She clutched the arms to her chair. "What do you mean?"

"It would take a bluestocking to inspire such tender feelings in the bosom of Dr. Fielding."

It was his mother's turn to laugh. "You have found me out. Clergymen have an unfortunate tendency to cram their daughters' heads with more knowledge than they can possibly use."

Robert offered no reply. As far as he could see, his mother had allowed her fine intellect to fall into complete disuse. He had never known her to read a book that carried any weight, nor hold a conversation that went too far beyond the gossip of the day.

She broke the silence. "Speaking of bluestockings, I met Gertrude Garwood at my mantuamaker's the other morning."

"Gertrude Garwood?"

"Of the Shrewsbury Garwoods. I happened to mention that Miss Garwood had been our guest at Linborough, and Gertrude denied ever having heard of her. What do you make of that, Robert?"

"I make nothing of it, Mother. Miss Garwood told me she

came from Bloomsbury. No mention was made of Shrewsbury."

"*Bloomsbury?* You mean in London?"

"I believe so."

"No girl of good family could possibly come from there. It is so—so—"

"Filled with mushrooms?"

"*Exactly!*"

"Some parts of Bloomsbury cannot even make that claim. The district is quite seedy in places."

"It is plain the girl is a fraud."

"She did not claim to be of consequence. In fact, I was given to understand that she is a penniless orphan whom the Marquess of Northwycke took under his wing out of the goodness of his heart."

"*Penniless?*" She shuddered. "My dear boy, it is lucky you did not pursue the idea of marrying the little nobody."

"Nevertheless the blood of three royal dynasties *does* flow through her veins. I would hardly call her a nobody."

"Pish-tosh. Any number of girls of good family can claim kinship to this king or that. I still say it was well done of you to see her off. Admit it, Robert, she does not measure up."

Robert affected surprise. "You think not?"

"Pray do not be ridiculous, dear. I do not care how many marquesses are willing to claim her as kin—her family could not possibly be good enough to marry into ours."

"In some ways, one could say that you and Miss Garwood think alike."

Robert watched her closely, not wishing to miss her reaction to this admission. To his delight, she took the bait. She had her cat-has-got-the-cream expression. So seldom did he manage to get the upper hand in their little exchanges.

"Well there you are. If even she agrees, what more need be said?"

"Forgive me, Mother, I did not make myself quite clear. Miss Garwood refused to marry me because to her way of thinking we Renquists do not measure up to *her* high standards."

"What?" The expression on her face was a mixture of

outrage and disbelief. "Well that settles it then. The girl must be deranged. Mark my words, our whole family has had a very fortunate escape."

"Perhaps it is she who is lucky to be rid of us. You see, I displayed a total lack of good breeding inasmuch as I questioned the suitability of her family with the very same breath I used to propose marriage to her."

His mother beamed. "And a jolly good thing you did. You did well to question her family. Such a bold creature would have made life miserable for all of us."

Robert stared at his mother in disbelief. Along with her title of duchess she had evidently assumed a mantle of omnipotence, for it was very clear she thought the Renquists could do no wrong. In a way, he pitied her for her lack of understanding.

"Come now, Mother. No one could make your life miserable. You are far too formidable."

Her eyes widened. "How could you even think that—much less say it? I am but a weak woman, with a mother's tender heart, but I would gladly sacrifice my life to ensure my family's happiness."

Robert gave her a placating pat. "The girls and I know that, Mother. I did not mean to imply otherwise. I suppose if I thought things through before speaking, I would have an easier time convincing some sweet young thing to marry me."

Seventeen

Lucy celebrated her seventeenth birthday in Venice in the palazzo of the Conte and Contessa Pavolini. The contessa, a girlhood friend of Lady Northwycke's, had fallen in love with and married the Italian nobleman on her very first trip to the Continent.

It was very clear to Lucy that she and her husband were still very much in love, thirty-two years later. Now in their early fifties, they still made an attractive couple. Her fair hair and blue eyes a striking contrast to his dark, graying hair and his liquid black eyes that shone like olives dipped in oil. Lucy was especially fascinated by the little signals they imparted to one another. The tiny caresses; the shared laughter, and the ardent glances that seemed to imply, *Later, my darling*.

The sexual tension the couple projected served to deepen Lucy's longing for Robert. Not that she would ever expect an English gentleman to display such passion in public, of course. But she had to own that she would not have objected if he had.

Lady Northwycke actually broached the subject one day when they were alone. They were going by gondola to the Rialto Bridge to do some shopping one afternoon when she said, "One cannot help noticing the shameful public display to which our hosts subject us. Of course, one expects it of the Italians, but good heavens, Edna is an *English* gentlewoman. It must be the climate. I can think of no other explanation."

"I can," Lucy replied wistfully. "I think they love one another very much."

Lady Northwycke reacted so strongly to her response that for a moment Lucy thought she was going to fall into the murky waters of the canal.

"*Love?* What has love got to do with base, animal passions?"

"Nothing, I should think. Perhaps love transforms such instincts into something wonderful."

The dowager's lips tightened into a thin line. "Lucy, that is balderdash. No amount of love can make the indignities a husband inflicts upon his wife's person seem wonderful. Where did you get such a dreadful idea?"

"The contessa."

"The *contessa?* How dare she defile the mind of a young girl? What exactly did she say to you?—that is if it does not offend your sensibilities to repeat it."

"She warned me against marrying an inept man."

"An inept man?"

"She told me that being made love to and listening to someone play the violin have a lot in common."

"What nonsense is this?"

"She said both experiences can be extremely unpleasant if performed by those lacking the proper skills."

Lady Northwycke turned purple. "Did she now? How dare she spout such indecencies to a young girl entrusted to my care? We shall not stay under her roof another day."

"Please, madam, are you sure you would wish to end a friendship of long-standing is such a manner? She meant no harm, and I have seen and heard far worse things at Hope House."

"Oh? Have you now? What sort of things, pray—if the staff there are conducting themselves in a manner—"

"No. Nothing like that," Lucy interjected hastily. "I was referring to the misery and abuse some of the little ones suffered before Cousin James came to their rescue."

Lady Northwycke nodded. "Perhaps you are right. I shall not make an issue of the matter, but we will be cutting our visit short. I shall say that we miss the family, and have decided to spend Christmas at home."

"I am so glad. Christmas anywhere else would not be the same."

Lady Northwycke looked thoughtful. "There is merit to what you say—about not making an issue of things. I suppose

Edna Purviance and I have been friends too long for me to wash my hands of her. But I must say, my feelings toward her have cooled, somewhat. The very idea—speaking to a young lady in such a manner."

They arrived in London two weeks before Christmas, but due to inclement weather had to wait at the house on Mayfair Court for several days before continuing their journey to Northwycke. To Lucy's surprise, on their third day in London Miles came to call on her.

As Miles nonchalantly leaned with his elbow on the mantel, sipping tea, Lucy could not help but admire the cut of his clothes. His growing prosperity added a certain sleekness to his dark, good looks. There was no doubt about it, she decided, Miles Walsingham was a very handsome man, and grew more so with each passing year.

Maude had told Lucy the story of how James had helped to raise him up from genteel poverty to his present state of being flush in the pocket by allowing him to invest ever-increasing amounts of money in the cargoes of his own trading ships.

Of all the male members of society Lucy had encountered over the years, she had to admit that Miles was the most handsome. She supposed that one of these days, some young lady of the *ton* would set her cap for him and it would be all over. She doubted the power of his resistance. Let it be someone who is as kind and thoughtful, she thought.

"How did you know we would be here?" Lucy asked.

"Emily mentioned in her last letter that you were expected, and with the weather being so foul, it did not take much effort on my part to assume you would be marooned here. Where is Lady Northwycke, by the way? Making the rounds this morning, visiting old friends and catching up on the latest gossip, I suppose?"

"Your supposition is way off the mark. Her ladyship retired to her bed right after breakfast. She found the trip from Italy to be most tiring."

"I should imagine. The lady is not getting any younger. She must be fifty, or thereabouts, would you not agree?"

Lucy frowned. "Really, Miles. Your speculations are most untoward. Her ladyship had better not hear you talk about her in such a disrespectful manner."

Miles affected a shudder. "I should hope not. As it is, she would just as soon I disappeared from the face of the earth. She bears no love for me."

Lucy was about to demur, but thought better of it "I must confess to having noticed that Lady Northwycke bears a certain animosity—no that is too harsh—a certain coolness toward you that finds me at a loss. You have always conducted yourself in a pleasant manner."

Miles laughed. "My dear girl, I could be the most pleasant chap in the world, and it would make no difference to the lady."

"But why, Miles?"

"Because I had the effrontery to fall in love with Maude. At the time Maude was too young to know any better and imagined she loved me back."

"Maude? Maude was in love with *you?*"

"Steady on there. Is that so hard to believe?"

"Of course not, Miles. I should imagine any number of young ladies would find you attractive."

"But not those of the Garwood family, it would seem."

"You said Maude had a *tendre* for you."

"But she was only fifteen, and it lasted all of five minutes."

He gave her a wistful look. "You know, I asked James's permission to offer for you, when you first came to live at Northwycke Hall."

"Realty? What was his answer?"

"He said I could propose to you as soon as you reached your sixteenth birthday."

"And now I am seventeen. Should I be hurt?"

Miles put down his cup. "Now then, Lucy, you know better than that. If I thought I had a chance, I would ask you to marry me in a heartbeat, but you are no longer the bewildered little waif I first met in the library at Northwycke Hall."

Lucy touched her throat. "I am not? Then who am I?"

"Damned if I know—do you?"

Lucy shrugged.

Miles gestured, "You have turned into a beautiful, self-assured young lady. Mind you, I always admired your looks, but now you are a diamond of the first water. Look at the dress you have on. No girl is turned out better."

Lucy unconsciously smoothed the layers of lace on what was a very lavish morning dress. "Lady Northwycke bought this for me in Italy. She is very generous."

"Open your eyes, Lucy. She has you confused with Maude."

"That is utter nonsense."

"Is it? Stop and consider. She took you to her bosom almost from the time Maude married Harcourt Langley, and be assured, Lucy, you will not escape from her clutches as easily as Maude. She is spinning a very tight web around you. One day you will wake up to find you have become a dried-up old spinster who is the companion of an even more shriveled old crone. Much good will pretty dresses from Italy do you then."

Lucy got up from her chair. "Miles, I have no wish to quarrel with you, but I think you had better go."

Miles looked dismayed. "Oh dear, that tears it. I've burned my bridges, have I not? I do not suppose you will ever speak to me again."

She touched his shoulder. "Of course I will, silly. Right now, I am quite out of sorts with you and might say something I most certainly would regret."

"May I call on you tomorrow, then?"

Lucy looked askance, then relented. "If you promise to behave, and refrain from such untoward remarks."

As soon as Miles had taken his leave, Lucy repaired to her chamber. Hoxie looked up from her sewing. "Forget something, did you, Miss Garwood?"

Lucy shook her head.

"Dull here, after Venice, isn't it?"

Lucy did not reply.

"The cold is perishing. I do miss all that lovely Italian sunshine."

"One would. Venice was very beautiful, but I am glad to

be back."

"Go on. Really, miss?" She handed her sewing to Lucy. "Here, I have mended the lace on this petticoat. My stitches still aren't as fine as yours, but I am improving."

Lucy went through the motions of inspecting her abigail's work. She looked up and smiled. "Yes. I see a distinct improvement. Thank you. I suggest you go below-stairs and treat yourself to a nice cup of tea."

Hoxie beamed. "If it is all the same to you, Miss Garwood, I think I will do just that."

When Hoxie left the room, Lucy picked up a looking glass and moved to the window. She took a long, hard look at her reflection. Was Miles right—had she become a diamond of the first water? Of a certainty, her features seemed to be stronger, no longer those of a child waiting for life to leave its imprint upon them. She thought she glimpsed a certain sadness reflected in her eyes. "Is that how we grow old and die?" she murmured. "One sorrow at a time?"

She put the looking glass down and shivered. What was it Miles had said? *Ah yes. One day I would become a dried-up old spinster whose sole purpose in life would be making sure an old hag did not lack for company. Those were not his exact words, but close enough.* She found them most unsettling.

Lucy did not receive Miles the next day. A watery sun broke through the clouds and fearing it might be a now-or-never sort of situation Lady Northwycke decided they should take a chance and head for home. As it turned out, it was the right decision, for the next morning the whole countryside was blanketed in snow.

Unfortunately, Maude could not be with them for Christmas, as she and her husband were spending the holiday in Yorkshire with his parents, the Earl and Countess of Larchville. To Lucy's surprise, Miles braved the weather and joined the family for the holidays. It seemed a positive sign for the festivities to be a success, but it did not make up entirely for Maude's absence.

On Christmas Eve, Lady Northwycke had the misfortune to slip on some ice and sustain a sprain to her right ankle. For the first few days, she hobbled around with the aid of a walking stick, but then took to leaning on Lucy's shoulder for support. No one gave this much thought; in fact, the family thought the bond that had developed between the two of them was rather touching.

On twelfth night, James and Emily invited several of the local families over to celebrate the end of Christmas. While the dowager was preoccupied with a game of whist, Miles took Lucy aside.

"Did I not warn you?" he said. "The lady spins a very strong web."

Lucy frowned. "Please, Miles. Do not let that feverish imagination of yours spoil a perfectly good party."

"Wake up, Lucy. Tell me, which ankle did she injure?"

"Her right one, of course. Why do you ask?"

"Because all this evening, she has been favoring her left one."

Lucy shrugged him off. "If you persist in your persecution of that dear lady, I shall refuse to have anything more to do with you."

Miles shook his head. "Very well, my dear, I will not utter another word, but I suggest you pay close attention and form your own conclusions."

"Thank you," Lucy snapped. "I will."

It was not until a Colonel Prescott, late of the Coldstream Guards, escorted Lady Northwycke into dinner that Lucy realized Miles had been speaking the truth. Maude's mother most decidedly favored her left leg.

Before Lucy departed for the Dower House, Miles took her aside. "Would you care to join me for a turn around the gardens tomorrow?"

"In the snow?"

"The paths have been cleared. Bundle up. The fresh air will do us both good."

"That is a splendid idea, Miles. Say, ten o'clock?"

Miles beamed. "I shall be knocking at your door."

Miles was as good as his word. The longcase clock in the hallway had not even begun to chime when Miles presented himself at the Dower House.

It was a crisp morning. The cold air stung Lucy's cheeks, so she covered the lower half of her face with a long woolen scarf. As they walked, no words passed between them. Lucy assumed that when Miles was ready to talk, he would do so, in the meantime, she listened to the chittering of sparrows in the nearby hedgerows.

Finally, Miles cleared his throat. "Lucy," he said. This was followed by a long silence, then he took a deep breath. "Lucy, I think you should marry me."

Lucy was at a loss. Not wishing to hurt his feelings with a refusal, she offered no reply.

"Dammit." Miles sounded frustrated. "I knew you would not jump at the idea, but hear me out Promise not to say a word until I have finished speaking."

Lucy patted his sleeve. "Miles, you have always been my friend, you have my word on that. I promise to keep quiet until you have spoken."

"Good. Well for a start, following James's advice, I have accumulated a sizable fortune and plan to reopen my house in Kent in a month or so."

"I am very happy for you."

Miles put his hand over her mouth. "Hush, you promised. It is about the third the size of Northwycke Hall, but is a handsome enough pile, I would say."

Lucy stopped walking. "Miles. If I loved you, I would gladly share a cottage with you."

"Lucy! Will you *please* listen? I think you should at least view your choices. The path you are now on takes you to a future of always living in someone else's house, reliant on the whims of another for every grace and favor, and always, always at their beck and call."

His repetition of the word "always" made her cringe. At first it had felt good to be mothered by Lady Northwycke, but like everything else in life, there was a price to pay.

Miles put an arm around her shoulder. "Please do not look so stricken, Lucy, I did not mean to upset you. Just bear with me. I am almost finished and I promise never to bring up the subject again."

Lucy nodded.

"I have seen how tenderly you handle the little ones at Hope House. You would make a wonderful mother. Just think, Lucy. Children of your own, to love and cherish, and above all, to educate. Think how much you would enjoy teaching them all the things you know. And last, but not least, as you pointed out, we *are* friends—not too many married couples can make that claim. I know you are not greatly enamored of me, but we would rub well together. Please consider it, Lucy. Surely the picture of you as Mrs. Walsingham, queen of your own household, is a more attractive one than that of Miss Garwood, spinster companion to the Dowager Marchioness of Northwycke?"

Lucy was touched by his sincerity. His proposal had not been tinged with the slightest hint of condescension or patronage. There had been no allusions to her doubtful lineage, just a sincere outreaching of one friend to another.

But what of passion? What mention was there of love?

Lucy dismissed the little voice in her head. After all, experience had taught her that with love and passion there was also pain. Did one ever get over such love? she wondered. Lady Northwycke had told her that in time she would. But so far, she had not felt any lessening of her sense of bereavement over parting with Robert. In contrast, Miles stood out as a beacon of comfort and safety.

Still mulling over her choices, she searched his eyes. They were filled with a mixture of hope and doubt. Dear, dear Miles. She removed her glove and stroked his cheek. "I would be honored to be your wife."

With a whoop he took her by the waist and swung her around. In his exuberance he lost his balance and landed in a snowbank with Lucy sprawled on top of him. They lay there for a moment, then they both started to giggle like small children.

He grabbed both ends of her scarf and pulled her face closer and planted a hearty kiss on her lips. By way of response, Lucy quickly kissed him back, and rolled off his body into the snow. There had been no magical transformation. Kissing Miles was still a rather pleasant experience—nothing more.

They both stood up and self-consciously brushed the snow off their clothes. Miles then gave her an awkward smile. "Well that is that, then." He gave her a quick hug. "Let's go tell the others. I know Emily will be tickled pink."

"It is comforting to know that least one of the Marchionesses of Northwycke will be happy for us, I wonder about the other?"

Miles laughed. "Please do not fret over it, Lucy. James helped send Napoleon running, I am sure he is well able to cope with his mother."

Lucy raised a brow. "You think so? I am of the opinion that if the lady had been in charge of our armies, the war would have been over far sooner."

"For shame, Lucy. You took me to task for saying far less about her."

"I know. I was just making light of the situation to lessen my anxiety. I happen to be very fond of Lady Northwycke."

Miles gave her elbow a squeeze. "I know that. The lady is a trifle outspoken, but she has a kind heart."

He linked arms with her. "Well. Who should we tell first, James and Emily, or the older Lady Northwycke?"

Lucy hesitated for a moment. "Neither. If it is agreeable to you, I should like Mickey to be the first one to know. Had he not brought me here, heaven knows what would have become of me."

Miles looked so surprised Lucy thought he was going to refuse, but he shrugged and said, "It is to the stables then. I have a feeling that marrying you is going to enlarge my social circle in the oddest way possible."

Mickey was walking two of the horses around the paddock when they got to the stables. He tipped his cap to Miles, then gave Lucy a questioning look.

"Good morning, Mr. Dempsey," Lucy said. "You remember Mr. Walsingham, do you not?"

Mickey cast Miles a suspicious glance. "I've taken care of 'is 'orse a time or two."

"I wanted you to be the first to know that Mr. Walsingham and I are going to be married."

Mickey beamed at Miles. "You are getting a good girl in Miss Lucy."

Lucy hoped Miles would understand her relationship with Mickey Dempsey, and not voice an objection to his familiarity. To her relief his face registered no sign of protest. Lucy was relieved, for had he done so, she might have been tempted to call off the engagement. She breathed easier when Miles smiled.

"I know that, Mr. Dempsey," he replied. "I promise to do everything in my power to make her happy."

Mickey wiped a tear from his cheek with the back of his hand. "Her poor mum and dad will rest easier for that."

"Yes," Lucy replied. "I like to think that is so. There are times I feel they are very close by." Her eyes began to tear. "Tell me, Mickey, how is Mrs. Dempsey faring? Well, I hope?"

Mickey's face lit up. "Very well. We are expecting a little one, come next summer."

"That is wonderful news. I know you will make a very good father."

Lucy exchanged a few more pleasantries, then they left for the Hall. They encountered James along the way. "Good morning," he said. "You two are up bright and early." His eyes then fixed on their linked arms. "Hello. Is there something I ought to know?"

It was Miles who answered. "Yes. Lucy has just agreed to marry me. I know I should have come to you first, but to be honest, I did not start out this morning with the faintest notion of asking her. The opportunity just seemed to present itself."

James smiled. "You probably did the right thing. Who knows? If you had waited until tomorrow, she might not have given you the same answer." He chucked Lucy under the chin. "I take it you were about to return to the Hall to break the news?"

They both nodded.

"Good. I shall accompany you, then. I was going to exercise Tarquin this morning, but it will keep. I would not miss the expression on Emily's face when you break the news to her for all the tea in China."

Emily did not disappoint them. She hugged and kissed them both, and laughed, then cried. Suddenly she stopped. "Do you realize what a mixed-up family we shall be? "Lucy will be our sister-in-law, as well as our niece."

Miles inserted, "I shall be your nephew-in-law, if such a title exists, as well as your brother. Please do not attempt to use the situation as an excuse to order me about."

Emily looked askance. "Much good would it do me. When have you listened to anything I have to say?" She smiled at Lucy. "You will find making Miles behave is an impossible task."

Instead of dismay, the dowager responded to the news of their engagement with an arch smile. "I suppose it was bound to happen—propinquity and all that. Only girl I know who would refuse a duke and accept a mister." She placed her hand on Lucy's shoulder. "You are probably doing the right thing. The curate's daughter would have gone out of her way to make your life miserable."

Eighteen

In February, the Northwyckes were invited to a house party in the neighboring parish of St. Giles. Their host, Wilfred Carruthers, better known as "Wiffey," was one of James's oldest and dearest friends. Along with Rodney Bonham Lewis, they had attended the same schools, and had fought in the same regiment on the Iberian Peninsula, so when Wiffey invited them to his house for a pre-Lenten ball, James accepted with alacrity.

Wiffey had inherited the estate from his father the previous year. The Carruthers were not a titled family, but were enormously rich. Wiffey's house was large, and James was encouraged to bring along as many members of his family as he chose. So James brought everyone, including Maude and Harcourt. The only one to stay at home was the youngest Garwood, James Elias.

The Garwoods arrived early in the evening, and along with about twenty others were served a meal described by their host as "just something to tide them over." It comprised of turtle soup, fish stuffed with other fish, veal, and chops with a remove of a huge joint of beef, and accompanying vegetables and pies filled with everything imaginable; followed by sorbets, and ending with fruit and Cheshire cheese stuffed with Stilton cheese—each course served with an appropriate wine.

Some of the gentlemen stayed behind to smoke cigars and drink brandy, but most of Wiffey's guests were only too happy to go to their bedchambers to nap before getting dressed for the ball later that night.

Lucy had picked sparingly at her food, but there had been so many courses, she felt uncomfortably full. Too full, in fact, to drop off to sleep. Instead, as she lay on the strange bed, she contemplated her engagement to Miles.

Far from being a passionate couple, the occasional kisses they shared could best be described as affectionate. She wondered if this was enough to sustain a marriage.

Of course not, you fool, her little voice said.

She sat up with a start and covered her face with her hands. "Dear heavens," she murmured. "What a coil I am in. I should never have listened to Miles."

Why not? the little voice taunted. *He offers you far more than you have a right to expect.*

Lucy pounded her forehead with her fists. "Leave me alone." She became deathly quiet and bit her lip. "Good heavens, I must be going mad."

She was brought to earth by a knock on her door. Hoxie entered. "Did you call me, miss?"

Lucy felt very foolish. "Er—yes. Is it not time for me to get dressed?"

Hoxie smiled. "It's a bit early, but we could get started. Who knows? Your hair may not behave and might have to be done over. More time is better than less, I always say."

Lucy's hair behaved very well, giving Hoxie plenty of time to experiment with it. When she was finished, Lucy stared in the mirror for a while, scarcely believing it was her own image staring back. Thick coils of her hair interwoven with gold ribbon sat atop the crown of her head. Curly tendrils framed her face and the nape of her neck.

"You may well stare," said Hoxie. "I have never seen you look more beautiful."

She dampened a red tissue and rubbed the dye on Lucy's lips. When her back was turned, Lucy wiped most of it off, leaving just a hint of color. Lucy spent the next half hour sitting in her petticoat before Hoxie deemed it time to put on her dress.

When she finally helped Lucy into her evening dress, Hoxie stood transfixed with admiration. It was a beautiful confection of white and gold, designed to subtly follow Lucy's curves. "The Italians make a lovely job of it. I'll wager none of the other ladies will be dressed as pretty."

As the finishing touch, Hoxie criss-crossed the laces of a

dainty pair of gold sandals halfway up the calves of Lucy's legs.

"You have the ankles for them, Miss Garwood. Hate to see that sort of thing on ladies with limbs the size of hams."

When Lucy entered the ballroom with the older Lady Northwycke, Emily immediately commandeered them. "Mother, guess who is here?"

The dowager shrugged, "I would not try to guess."

"Cecily. Cecily Tyndall. Can you believe that? I have invited her to several of our soirees only to be told she was staying with her uncle's family in Jamaica."

"Really? I have never met the girl. The very least she could have done was to write to you to acknowledge your kind invitations."

Emily laughed. "Cecily was not the most apt pupil, I would not expect her to respond. I wrote a letter to her once, but I fear it was misdirected. She told me it did not arrive. In any case, as soon as I catch sight of her again, I should like to present her to you both."

"You show more forbearance than I would. She seems to be very careless of her friendships," Lady Northwycke said.

Emily laughed. "I suppose so, but we grew up together, and I find it hard to part with friends of long-standing."

The dowager peered through the crowd. "Which one is she? As I recall, you described her as thin."

"That is the most marvelous part, Mother. She was as thin as a sparrow and was cursed with a blotchy complexion, but she has become a beauty."

Emily stopped short and gave Lucy an assessing look. "My goodness, I was so busy rattling on I did not take notice of what you had on. Lucy, you look like one of those goddesses come down from Mount Olympus."

"Yes," Lady Northwycke inserted, "I was just telling her so."

"You are also a picture of elegance, Mother. The silver sets your coloring off to perfection."

The dowager bloomed. "Do you really think so, my dear?"

"Yes, indeed, Mother, I do," Emily replied most earnestly. "But then, you are always the epitome of grace, and style."

"Thank you, Emily. How very kind of you to say so." She punctuated this remark with a tiny flutter of her fan.

"What about you, Emily?" Lucy inserted. "You look very lovely yourself. The green of that dress does magical things to your eyes, and those magnificent diamonds and emeralds are fit for a queen."

Emily fingered the stones of her necklace. "These were a gift from James. I have only worn the dress or the emeralds but once. It was to a ball the Fotheringhams hosted, as a matter of fact." She smiled. "We were newly married and on our return home I picked a terrible fight with James. I almost ruined our marriage."

Lucy found it hard to believe such a thing of sweet-natured Emily.

Emily beckoned to a young lady in a pale blue dress. Then he pulled Lucy and the dowager forward with her to meet her halfway. While Emily made the introductions, Lucy took the measure of the other girl.

Cecily Tyndall lacked the inches that she and Emily enjoyed, but Lucy had to own that she was well proportioned and had a pleasing figure. If her complexion had once been blotchy, as Emily described, there was no sign of it now. Her face was the perfect blend of cream and roses. Her hair was golden, rather than flaxen, but it was her eyes that held Lucy's attention. They were the same pale blue as her dress. She had never seen such compelling eyes before. They had a mesmerizing quality she found most unsettling.

Lucy was relieved when Cecily Tyndall made her curtsy and moved on to greet other people of her acquaintance. The number of those attending the ball swelled as members of the local gentry began to arrive. By midnight, it was a very 'sad' crush indeed!

The strains of a waltz floated down from the musician's gallery, and Miles came to claim it. After having made the effort to look beautiful for him, Lucy was piqued when he did not even bother to compliment her on her appearance.

She danced with several other gentlemen, including James,

and Maude's husband, Harcourt. Once she saw Miles dancing with Cecily Tyndall, then lost sight of him for a while.

When she was between dances, he finally joined her and they sat together, watching the others go through the sets of a quadrille. Miles seemed preoccupied. Lucy had the feeling he was not really there at all. As if he had departed his body and left an empty husk by her side.

When they took their leave of their host the next afternoon, Miles departed for London, while the rest of the family returned to Northwycke Hall. Lucy was not sorry to see him go. He had seemed pensive and unapproachable every time they were thrown together.

There was a bright side to it all. Maude and Harcourt were going to stay with the family for a whole week before returning to their country seat in Sussex. Even so, the pleasure she derived from Maude's company was marred by the knowledge that the Saturday after Easter she was supposed to marry Miles at St. Cuthbert's.

Early in March, Miles declared his house in Kent open for inspection. James could not leave his affairs in London to make the journey, and since James Elias had a case of the sniffles, Emily did not choose to go. The dowager declined the invitation, complaining the damp weather was causing too much pain to her ankle. That left Lucy, Maude, and Harcourt.

Oakwood was a charming manor house, not large, compared to some, but it was obvious Miles had put considerable time and money into restoring the place to its former glory.

Their first morning Miles took Harcourt to ride the boundaries of the estate. Maude and Lucy chose to walk in the gardens. They both laughed on espying a newly installed rose arbor.

"I am wagering the roses will be white."

Lucy inhaled sharply. She felt as if she had been stabbed through the heart. "You are probably right," she replied, trying to keep her voice as neutral as possible.

"Oh my dear!" Maude exclaimed. "That was terribly thoughtless of me. It is only natural that you would still have *some* regard for Robert Renquist."

Lucy did not reply. Indeed, could not. She felt as if there were a lead weight on her chest.

Maude pointed out a neglected herb garden. "Once you are mistress here, Lucy, you will really enjoy yourself setting that to rights. You are always at your happiest when you have your hands in the soil."

These words were the final straw. They opened a floodgate of tears that Lucy could not control.

Maude held her close, and while patting her back, crooned, "There, there, Lucy. It is all right."

Gradually, Lucy's crying subsided into convulsive sobs.

Maude looked contrite. "My dear Lucy, I did not mean to cause all that."

Lucy waited to gather her composure before making a reply. "It is not you, Maude. It is just that the thought of marrying Miles and being mistress of this house fills me with despair. I think it is plain to see that I do not love Miles. I am in love with Robert Renquist."

"Then you must tell Miles that you cannot possibly marry him."

"I will not do that to him. He is too fine a person."

"But if he learns you do not love him, I am sure he will not wish to go through with the wedding."

"He knew I was not greatly enamored of him—his words, incidentally—when he proposed to me. There is no passion in our kisses. I do not think Miles is even aware there should be."

"How awful."

"He is perfectly content with the arrangement. In fact, he asked James's permission to marry me before I even had my fifteenth birthday."

Maude stepped back. "He did *what*? That is beyond everything. What was James's response?"

"He told him he could ask me when I turned sixteen."

"How very good of him."

191

"Please do not criticize your brother, Maude. He only did what he thought was best."

"I wonder why Miles waited so long to propose to you?"

"He did not think I would have him."

"No," Maude replied. "He waited until you were more vulnerable and unable to think straight. Lucy, you do not owe him all this consideration."

"Please, Maude. I beg of you."

"It is fortunate that you decided against making your engagement public. I think you both should reconsider this marriage. You will only make each other miserable."

"That is up to Miles. I would not hurt him for the world."

"Something should be done about it."

"Please, Maude, promise me you will not mention any of this to Miles."

"This is sheer folly."

"Promise."

"Very well, Lucy, I promise."

A week later, Robert came to Town to prepare his house for the Season. There were minor repairs to the structure, winch needed to be addressed, and he took the head gardener to task over the condition of some of the flowerbeds.

After one frustrating afternoon, when anything that *could* go wrong did, he sought refuge in his library with a book, and a cup of a particularly fine blend of Turkish coffee. He was just beginning to settle down when a servant bearing the news that a Lady Langley wished to speak to him disturbed his peace.

"What the devil? Put her ladyship in the green room and offer her some refreshments. I shall have to change my clothes before I receive her."

He grumbled all the way to his chambers. "Damned inconvenient. Dropping in like that. A man is not free to relax in his own house."

He rinsed his face in water, and combed his hair, then changed his old jacket for something newer and less comfortable, all the time wondering what Maude Garwood could possibly want of him that would make her fly in the face of convention. The very idea, coming to a gentleman's house unescorted!

As he came down the stairs, he wondered if something had happened to Lucy. The thought made his heart skip a beat.

Then reason prevailed. James Garwood would have broken the news himself. This bought him back full circle—what could Maude Garwood possibly want of him?

He walked into the drawing room, a polite smile on his face, and bowed. "Ah. My dear Lady Langley," he said in his most urbane manner. "How do you do?"

Maude dropped him a curtsy. "How do you do, Your Grace?"

He offered her a chair, an elegant French confection of pale blue tapestry, and sat down facing her in a slightly more substantial one, upholstered in a green and blue brocade.

Robert had no inclination to go through the ritual of asking after the welfare of every member of her family, so he got right to the point. "Lady Langley, why are you here? Is something the matter with Miss Garwood?"

"If you are asking if Lucy is ill, the answer is no. But is something the matter? I would have to say everything is, and it is mostly your fault."

Robert felt his hackles rise. "What the devil do you mean by that, Maude?"

"Good. I have made you angry enough to forget all the silly formalities. Now, perhaps we may get to the heart of the matter."

"Which is?"

"Lucy is going to marry Miles Walsingham in April, eleven o' clock in the morning, the Saturday following Easter at St. Cuthbert's in Northwycke."

Robert felt his throat constrict. "That has nothing to do with me."

"It has *everything* to do with you. For some reason I have been unable to fathom, she is hopelessly in love with you."

"I find that hard to believe."

"I agree. After the shameful way you treated her, it is beyond all comprehension, is it not?"

"Stop this sparring, Maude. If she loves me, why would she marry Walsingham? It does not make sense."

"When Miles asked her to marry him, he did so with respect. He did not try to strip away her pride by denigrating her family." Maude spoke slowly, as if trying to get her point across to someone a trifle dense. "Lucy is every bit as proud as you are. When you belittled her parentage, you gave her no choice but to refuse you."

"Maude, what point are you trying to make?"

"If you love her, you will straighten out this coil. Lucy is miserable without you. You cannot let her marry Miles. You have to stop her. Perhaps speak with him—or carry her off on that great white horse of yours—think of *something*, for pity's sake—*anything*. Miles will get over it. He is a nice man, but not given to deep feelings."

Maude made this delivery without drawing a single breath, then slumped in her chair when she had finished, as if exhausted by the effort.

Robert stood up. "Maude, for your sake, I am going to forget that this preposterous little scene ever took place. I know you mean well, but I do not choose to subject myself to any more of this. I think you should leave, and hope to heaven no one saw you enter. It would make fine grist for the gossip mill."

Maude stood up. Her passion evidently spent, she meekly replied, "My apologies, Your Grace. I shall take up no more of your time." She curtsied and departed, leaving him to stew over her words.

"Damn you, Maude," he muttered, all hope for a peaceful afternoon shattered.

Not wishing to be left alone to brood over the matter, he ordered a carriage to be sent round, then changed his clothes once more. This time, he wore something suitable for an evening at White's, where he imbibed a considerable amount of brandy, and contrary to his nature, lost a tidy sum at gaming.

• • •

Miles did not join the family for Easter services, pleading a lack of time. He wanted to add a few more finishing touches to the house before bringing his bride there.

Lucy watched the parishioners file into the church on Easter Sunday from the vantage point of the family pew. They had decided against having wedding banns posted in favor of marrying by special license. As James put it, "The less others know about one's business, the better."

Her scalp tightened. Next Saturday, she would be standing before the altar, promising to be Miles Walsingham's wife until the day one of them died. She wondered how James and Emily would react if she were to call it off? She had broached the subject with Emily, once, but was assured that she was merely suffering from a case of prenuptial jitters.

"Did you?" Lucy had asked.

Emily had laughed. "I was whisked to the altar before I had time to realize what was happening."

After the service, Lucy wandered around the churchyard, while the rest of the Garwoods conversed with some of the local gentry. Lucy read the legends on the gravestones, and wondered about the people behind the names. They had lived and loved, perhaps hated, most certainly laughed and cried. Now, they were dust.

"A sobering sight, is it not?"

Lucy started at the sound of the girlish voice and found herself staring into the pale, blue eyes of Cecily Tyndall.

"Good morning, Miss Tyndall, I did not see you in church."

"I was in the Partinger pew. Sir John is my uncle."

"I have met your aunt and uncle at various functions and have found them to be most agreeable."

"It is good of you to say so, Miss Garwood."

This exchange of pleasantries was followed by an awkward silence. Lucy noticed that the blue taffeta lining the bonnet of the other girl seemed to intensify the color of her eyes, yet the effect was no less disconcerting than the paler blue she had worn at Wiffey Carruther's ball.

"You must pay a call to Northwycke Hall while you are in

the district, otherwise my cousins will be most disappointed."

Cecily Tyndall gave her a wry smile. "I doubt I would be welcome."

Lucy felt at a loss. "Please explain, Miss Tyndall. It is very clear that you are not here to discuss the weather."

"No, Miss Garwood, I am not."

"Oh? Perhaps we should take a stroll."

They left the church grounds through the lych-gate and turned left down the lane. After a couple of hundred yards or so, Cecily Tyndall stopped. "This is far enough, my shoes are not too comfortable."

Lucy was expecting her to add something to the statement, but then the other girl subjected her to yet another embarrassing silence.

Lucy lost her patience. "Miss Tyndall, if you have something to say to me, kindly do so."

"You must not marry Miles," she said. Her voice was so soft, Lucy was not quite sure she heard aright, "He is in love with me."

"I see." On the one hand, Lucy felt betrayed, on the other, she experienced a great rush of relief. "I suppose this love unfolded at Mr. Carruther's ball?"

Cecily Tyndall nodded.

"How did it come about? Did he kiss you?"

The other girl colored. "It was quite the reverse. I have always had a *tendre* for Miles, but I might have waited forever for him to kiss me first." She bit her lip. "Had I known of your betrothal, I would not have dreamed of doing so."

"That would have been a pity, for I assume the kiss was wonderful?"

Her eyes widened, "You are not angry?"

Lucy shook her head. "Perhaps a little. I cannot imagine what possessed Miles to continue our engagement when it is you he loves. I am assuming that he, too, took great delight in this kiss?"

"He gave me reason to believe so."

Lucy patted her arm. "I am sure he was sincere. You see

he has not been the same since that night. In fact, I have been having serious doubts about marrying him."

Cecily Tyndall's eyes filled with hope. "Then I am given to understand that you will call this wedding off?"

"Of course not! The very idea. Emily has gone to *far* too much trouble for us to do that."

"*Oh.*" She sounded devastated.

"The wedding *must* take place, but with a different bride. No one outside of the family will even know."

Cecily Tyndall's brows shot up. "Is it possible to do such?"

"If your father is agreeable."

She clapped her hands. "Yes. Yes. My father is very *fond* of Miles, and what is more, denies me nothing which is in his power to give."

"If this is the case, ask him to be so kind as to procure a special marriage license. The wedding is scheduled for next Saturday, at eleven o' clock."

Cecily Tyndall sighed. "Yes, I know."

"You have all of Miles's particulars? His age and date of birth—that sort of thing?"

"Yes, yes. Yes, I have made it my business to do so. You see, I have known Miles since I was in leading strings." She flung her arms around Lucy, then pulled back, her eyes filled with panic. "Are you sure this will work?"

"Miss Tyndall, try not to worry. Miles will be told what has transpired, and you *are* his sister's dearest friend, so there should be no objections from that quarter. All that is left for you to do is to arrive at the church at the appointed time."

Until she revealed to him what she had done, Lucy was not aware that James had a temper. He used a lot of phrases to express his displeasure. Before he had finished, Lucy was well aware that she had "taken too much upon herself…" and "had the effrontery to…" By the time he was finished, she was in tears. However, Emily suggested sending couriers with letters to both Cecily's father and Miles, and to James's surprise, both were amenable to the idea.

Of course, it was to the Tyndall family's advantage to have

Cecily marry Miles. Mr. Tyndall was not exactly flush in the pocket. Miles's newly acquired prosperity, plus his connection to the Garwoods, constituted an advantageous match for his daughter.

The Tyndalls declined an invitation to stay at Northwycke Hall for the wedding eve, electing to stay with the Partingers. Lady Partinger was Mrs. Tyndall's sister, and having fared better in the marriage mart than her sibling, lived in a handsome manor house on the other side of Northwycke. Naturally, Miles stayed at the Hall.

The sun shone brightly on the day of the wedding, without a hint of any forthcoming April shower. It was a private affair, with only relatives of both families in attendance. The bride and groom had eyes only for one another, and Cecily had to be prompted to produce the ring for Miles to hand over to the minister. This resulted in a ripple of laughter among family members.

Lucy joined in the laughter. *Cecily loves Miles the way I love Robert*, she thought.

Then why did you make it so easy for him to walk away?

"Because I am a proud, stubborn fool," she murmured to herself.

"I did not quite catch what you said," Emily whispered.

"'Twas nothing," she whispered back. "I merely remarked that they looked well together."

Emily patted her hand and returned her attention to the bride and groom.

The minister was about to pronounce the couple man and wife when suddenly the doors of the church flung open and a shaft of sunlight streamed in. All heads spun around, including those of the bridal couple. In the blinding light, the silhouette of a very large man was outlined in the doorway.

Lucy's heart skipped a beat. That powerful frame could only belong to one man. She got up from her seat and held her breath as she watched him stride down the aisle, the muscles in his thighs very much in evidence within the confines of his well-tailored pantaloons.

He came to a halt halfway to the altar, and with his feet squarely placed, said, "I hope I am not too late to—" He stopped short. It was plain he had taken note of the golden ringlet peeking from beneath the white bonnet the bride wore.

He bowed to Cecily, who gazed at him openmouthed. "Forgive the intrusion. I seemed to have made a mistake."

He turned to go.

Lucy scrambled over James's feet to get out of the pew. "No, Robert. Wait!"

He turned around. *It was not enough for her to humiliate me,* he thought. *She has to be here to deliver the final blow.* Then she threw herself at him, her eyes reflecting the longing that tormented his every waking hour. He had been about to repudiate her, but realized it was not in him to do so.

He resigned himself to the inevitable. Come what may, Lucy Garwood was in his life to stay, because he could not imagine living without her. He motioned to the minister. "Kindly proceed with the ceremony." Then oblivious to the gasps of those in attendance, he scooped Lucy into his arms, and carried her out of the church.

He deposited her in his curricle, climbed in beside her, then scowled. "If you wanted a reconciliation, Lucy, why did you not just write me a letter? Was it absolutely necessary to send Maude to my house to make a complete cake of me, with that cock-and-bull story about you marrying Miles today?" He shook his head. "You may be sure he will not be thanking you for ruining his wedding day."

Lucy folded her arms and glowered. "I am not responsible for Maude's lunacy, whatever that may be. But had I not stepped down at the last minute to allow Cecily Tyndall to take my place, you would have witnessed the leg-shackling of the unhappiest couple ever to kneel before an altar."

Robert moved to embrace her, but she stood up and started to climb out of the carriage.

He grabbed her wrist. "Please, why are you leaving?"

She looked down her nose at him. "Because I am not well pleased with you, sir. It just occurred to me that you did not get here any too soon. That is hardly flattering."

He pulled her to him. "Get back here, you little minx." He loosened the strings of her bonnet and removed it from her head. Her hair gleamed like copper in the sunlight. He ran his fingers through it and touched a strand to his lips. He trailed his fingers down her face, then kissed her eyelids.

"How I have missed you."

"And I, you," she murmured.

Robert caressed her collar, which buttoned to the hollow of her throat. "I love the way you look in blue. You wore it the very first time we kissed."

His gaze dropped to the hem of her skirt, which in her attempt to leave the curricle had been disarranged. "Good heavens, Lucy, you have *lace* on your petticoats. Oceans of it. I have it on good authority that any self-respecting bluestocking would not *dream* of wearing so much lace on her pantalettes, so I assume the same theory would apply to petticoats."

Lucy straightened her dress. "I doubt but few ladies wear pantalettes these days, but who made such an absurd statement, pray?"

Robert laughed. "The authority on bluestockings. The eminent Dr. Fielding, of course."

"Ha! You would take the word of such a man? I wager the last woman he kissed was his own mother."

Robert cleared his throat. "Actually, that distinction probably belongs to *my* mother."

"*Dr. Fielding?*"

Robert nodded. "To the point of suffocation, I am led to believe."

"*Really?* How does one do that?"

"Like this." He took her in his arms and claimed her lips.

They did not notice when the church emptied of people, or hear all but one carriage drive away. It took a sudden April shower to end the kiss. Then he was moved to kiss away the raindrops running down her cheeks.

"I love you so very much," he murmured. "But, my beautiful nymph, never more than when you are soaking wet."

Suddenly, Robert felt a hand on his shoulder. The Marquess of Northwycke loomed over the curricle like an avenging angel. "You had better have a special license bearing my niece's name," he said sternly. "Otherwise, old chap, I will have no choice but to call you out." He softened the threat with the merest trace of a smile.

Robert reached into his breast pocket and fished out the required document.

"Good. Now would you like to name the day? From all appearances, I would say, the sooner, the better."

"Your parson would not happen to be still hanging about the premises, would he?"

"As luck would have it, the parson, my wife, *and* my mother all await inside."

Robert put his arm around Lucy and gave her guardian the wickedest of grins. "In that case, Uncle James, Lucy and I both agree with you, sooner is far, far better."

Also by Mona Prevel

The Dowager's Daughter

Affairs of the state will soon give way to affairs of the heart.

Althea Markham shoulders many burdens of being an unattached countess—wading through the collection of gold-diggers and rogues to find a suitable husband, providing her family with a male hair, and most of all, protecting her mother, who tends to acts more debutante than dowager. As she sneaks away for illicit meetings with a mysterious stranger, Althea is determined to unveil his identity—and his intentions.

Desperate to escape from beneath the shadow of his older brother, John Ridley takes part in a daring game of espionage against the French. Posing as a smuggler, he engages with the charming Celeste Markham. But despite her winsome allure, it is her daughter, Althea, who seizes John's attention.

As affairs of the state give way to affairs of heart, John must convince Althea that she can trust him with her future, and her love.

Educating Emily

He taught her the ways of the world, and she taught him the ways of love.

Fated to be sold into a loveless marriage, Emily Walsingham runs away. But when she is rescued by dashing James Garwood, she fall desperately in love. Recognized by James's mother, Emily is declared the perfect wife for him, despite the fact that he has yet to declare his love for her.

When James Garwood agrees to marry Emily, he never expected to be any more than a tolerable companion. But as she proves to be more caring and intelligent than he imagined, a man thought to be incapable of true devotion will learn more than he bargained for about falling in love.

The Love-Shy Lord

Their match was impossible, but their love was inevitable.

Too tall for a society woman, Clarissa has no potential suitors—not that she needs any. She only has eyes for Marcus, viscount of Fairfax. But as a steward's daughter, Clarissa is hardly a suitable match for Marcus.

Marcus Ridley is far too appealing—and eligible—for his own good. Restlessly pursued by desperate maidens, his view of women and marriage is skewed. But then he meets Clarissa, who steals his heart with a single kiss.

Suddenly, Marcus can't get Clarissa off of his mind, and the high-society lord finds himself desperate to make the steward's daughter his wife.